Stories for the Weekend

Antoinette N. Wood

The stories contained in this collection are fictional. Any resemblance to persons living or dead or situations is purely coincidental.

Published by Antoinette N. Wood

ISBN 978-0-6151-8687-0

Library of Congress Control Number

2008900949

About the Author

Antoinette N. Wood was born in Newark, NJ in 1980. She is an avid reader and has been writing short stories since age 8. She formed a writing club with her friends in fifth grade called *The Young Writers Club* (disbanded in 1991). She continued to write throughout high school, publishing a few pieces in the school's literary magazine. She is currently the editor of *The Red Rabbit,* an online literary journal, and *Fat Girl Magazine,* a size-positive, size acceptance online magazine for full-figured women.

She currently lives in New Jersey with her two cats, Grace and Oliver and is happily engaged to her boyfriend of three years.

Stories

Estrangement

I was holding my baby in my arms while my husband stood in front of me and told me that his staying someplace else for a while was the right thing to do. Just for a little while, he kept saying. Just so he could be closer to work and get some sleep because the baby kept crying all night and waking him up. He was holding the black plastic handle of his rolling suitcase in his left fist. In his right hand he held his cell phone. I stared at them alternately and tried to piece together in my mind what he was trying to say.

Behind me I could hear the tea kettle screaming in the kitchen. The television was playing loud enough to drown out all the ambient sound. I became aware of my clothes, *his* clothes I should say. His oversized t-shirt, his baggy sweatpants and his ratty old moccasins. I smelled like baby vomit and my face was orange and green from splatters of baby food. The baby was playfully yanking on a strand of my hair but I couldn't feel it. All I felt was numb.

My husband was wearing khakis with a crease down the front. His brown leather shoes were still shiny, like he'd just taken them out of the box. He probably had because I'd never seen those shoes before.

He was wearing a dark blue button down and a leather camel colored

jacket. He smelled like some new cologne. His beard was trimmed, his

haircut was sharp and his glasses were clean. He didn't even have

blackheads on his nose. His lips were glossy from some honey flavored

balm that I could smell all the way across the room. He was fairly

glowing while he stood there and told me he needed to get more sleep.

Over his shoulder I could see through the front window beside

the door. I could see over our frost covered lawn to the curb where his

car was parked. He hadn't pulled into the driveway. The windows

were steamed. The car was still running.

He'd come in about ten minutes before. He kissed my cheek,

picked up the baby and made little noises in her face while she

squirmed and chortled away. I started yapping as soon as he got in the

door. Mary came by earlier to bring some apple turnovers she made.

She was telling me about her grandson who's in pre-school. What do

you think the baby will be like by that time?

He didn't know, he said.

Well, Mary's grandson is very precocious. Whatever that

means. Oh, and the guy came by to fix the water heater but I told him

he should come back and speak to you when you were home because I

don't know what's wrong with it. Um, what else? You forgot to write a

check for the cable. The one we sent out for the phone bounced. By like two dollars. That was my fault though. I shouldn't have charged a coffee to my card.

"Kelly?" he said.

I kept on talking. "I didn't cook. I just didn't get time to. I fell asleep when I put Alexis down for her afternoon nap and we just woke up an hour ago. I was just about to have tea when I heard the car pull up. Want some? Can you take the garbage out when you get settled? I want to start dinner. Do you want chicken or pork chops?"

Then I realized that I was the only one talking. I turned around with a pack of frozen pork chops in my hand and stared at my husband in the doorway of the kitchen. He was watching me and not speaking and barely blinking. I dropped the pork chops on the counter and the noise startled the baby in the living room. She wailed.

Kelly, he'd said. I need to talk to you.

After he said what he'd come home to say, he went upstairs and started packing a few things. I stayed in the kitchen, still hovering somewhere between shock and confusion. They both pressed down on my head until I felt like I was an inch off the floor. Then I was propelled to move. Out of the kitchen. Into the living room. Pick up the baby. Run up the stairs. Push open the door. Stop him.

"What are you doing?" I asked him. "I don't understand."

Just for a little while. Too much pressure at work. Couldn't

deal with pressure at home too. He needed to relax his mind.

Alexis started to bawl and I shook her gently to get her to be

quiet. I didn't want to hear any other sounds. All I wanted to hear was

his voice so I would know every word that he was saying. I couldn't

miss a single word.

He took the time to fold everything he put in the suitcase. He

went into the bathroom and came out with a handful of toiletries. He

took the book he'd been reading off the bedside table, *Modern Medical

Miracles and the Doctors Who Performed Them*, and tossed it in the

suitcase. His cologne followed that into the suitcase. Finally, he took

the framed photo of our daughter off the dresser and placed it on top.

He looked at me as he turned to leave. His eyes looked

resigned, frustrated and not in the mood for any silly temper tantrums

I meant to throw because of this. He hadn't said he was leaving for

good. Just for a few weeks to catch up on some sleep. He was a doctor.

He could fall asleep in surgery and someone might die. He couldn't

miss a beat during rounds and one silly oversight could mean the end

of his career, this house, this neighborhood. I had to understand that he

was only looking out for all of us. Not just himself. Sleep was the way

he could do that. And he couldn't sleep here with us. His family.

When he'd gotten to the bottom of the stairs, I stopped him. I said please. I begged him not to do this. That we could find some other way. He just stood there, looking at me as he had since he'd come into the house. Drowned and pathetic and wearing his clothes, I got no sympathy.

Then his cell phone rang. We both stood very still. Slowly he reached into his pocket and looked at the display screen. For a moment so brief I almost missed it, a little smile hitched up the corners of his mouth before dropping them again. He pressed a button and put the phone to his ear.

"Hi…yeah…okay. No, it's cool…We said seven thirty, right?" He laughed. "See you then. Bye."

He kept the phone in his hand after he ended the call. His mouth formed a thin line across the lower half of his face. His shoulders hunched a little and he took a step back.

"Well…" He reached for the door. "I'll call you, okay?"

My eyes burned as he continued to back away. I felt a hand on my back, pushing me forward.

"Wait—``

"I can't stay, Kelly. I have dinner plans."

What about our dinner? I wanted to shout. But I said nothing. I watched through the window as he trudged over the lawn, put his suitcase in the trunk and climbed into his SUV. Then he was gone.

It all happened so quickly, like a band aid being snatched off. Funny how that's supposed to hurt less but it still stings like a bitch. The night after Malcolm left, I just kept going about my regular activities as though he'd just said he had to do graveyard shift at the hospital and wouldn't be home. I fed Alexis, I put her to bed. I cleaned and ate dinner in front of the television. I went up to bed a little before midnight and fixed the pillows beside me like I usually do when he's not there.

When I woke up that next morning, it was like nothing had happened. The sky was overcast and fairly pulsing with the threat of rain. I got up and opened the window a little and breathed in the cold air. I just stood there for a while staring down my street. All the driveways were empty, the street was quiet. Alexis was still asleep in her room. I felt completely alone but I was calm. After a while, I got dressed so I could run some errands.

I drove through town with Alexis strapped in her car seat. It was mindless driving though. I didn't even know what errands I had to run. I just knew I needed to get out of the house, to breathe in some other kind of air. It didn't seem to be working but I kept driving anyway. I waved to Mrs. Turtle as she came out of Starbucks. I tooted my horn at the Mercer boys who were skating around the town square and called out to Reverend O'Shaughnessy who was conversing with my neighbor Mary and her daughter-in-law on the steps of our church.

I hadn't realized that I'd pulled into the parking lot at the supermarket. I guess sometimes if you just let yourself go, you'll end up going in the right direction. I shopped with a smile on my face, although I don't know what I was so pleased about. I was treating that shopping trip like it was one of my greatest joys. I suppose I was just desperate to not think of the night before.

I inspected each piece of fruit or vegetable I put into my cart. When I spotted a pumpkin bin I was so excited I practically raced over to it. See, I used to carve pumpkins with my brother when we were kids and it always made me feel pretty good, like I was home and everything was normal. I was bending over the edge to pull one of the bigger ones from the bottom out when I glanced up and saw her.

She was knocking on cantaloupes. I knew she saw me too because she paused for a moment. I could see she didn't want to smile at me but she had to because she knew my husband had left me.

"Hi, Kelly. How are you holding up?" she asked, smiling with her mouth instead of her eyes.

Fine, I'd said.

She looked down at my clothes. I was wearing stained jeans and a flannel shirt I'd pilfered from a Salvation Army donation box back in college six years ago. I was still wearing clothes that hadn't even been stylish anymore six years ago.

She — Tyra — had on soft chocolate pants that fit just right around her big hips and wrapped themselves tightly around her thighs. She was wearing open-toed gold heels that bunched all her toes together. She wore this expensive-looking leather jacket that she'd zipped all the way up. Her hair looked light and healthy and swayed from the breeze when someone walked by. Her face was flawless with makeup. She looked like a catalog model. I was still college grunge.

"Is this the baby?" she asked as she reached out to touch her.

I moved the cart away. "Yes, this is Alexis."

"Malcolm talks about her so much. You'd think the sun rose and set on her."

"It does," I said somewhat indignantly.

Whatever amusement that caught fire in her eyes had quickly died. She smirked a little and sighed and said, "He's okay."

What do you mean "he's okay"? I asked her.

"Malcolm," she said. "Malcolm's all right. He just…he needed his rest, Kelly."

I cringed at hearing her say my name. Then I looked down at

the pumpkin and suddenly my urge to go home and carve it out and

roast pumpkin seeds seemed stupid and childish. Tyra Bettani

wouldn't go home and roast pumpkin seeds. She'd go home and run a

hot bath and sip a California merlot. She'd listen to jazz or orchestral

music. She'd eat sophisticated dinners like asparagus with buttery

hollandaise and a juicy filet mignon with sprigs of rosemary and

parsley to garnish. She'd probably work out right after because she

wouldn't want a thing like beef to settle on her hips. Then she'd lie

down on satin sheets and fall asleep right away because she was not

waiting for a baby to cry.

"How do you know that?"

"I had dinner with him last night," she said.

She had dinner with my husband last night while he was

supposed to be at home having dinner with me. I gripped the handle of

my shopping cart and started to walk away but her voice stopped me.

"You should try to make things easier for him."

I whipped around. I wanted to say something awful to shut

her up. I wanted her to stop pretending like she knew my husband and

our relationship better than I did. But I couldn't think of anything so I

turned my cart and marched down the dairy aisle.

When I joined the checkout line, she was in the lane across from me. I could feel her looking at me, wanting me to turn and look at her. I tried to close my mind of anything involving her. She didn't exist to me. She was just some pretentiously dressed woman at the supermarket pushing her cart with hardly a thing in it. I scoffed at her and I hoped she saw it.

I put my few items on the belt and handed the cashier my credit card. She was paying for her purchases across from me and I took the opportunity to give her a nasty stare. Then the cashier tapped me on the shoulder and said, "This is declined."

I dug in my wallet and handed her another one. "This one is declined too."

There was no cash in my wallet. I didn't have my checkbook. I was stuck at the front of a long line with no money and I was so embarrassed.

"Here, let me take care of that."

She came charging over with a handful of cash extended toward the cashier.

"No," I said sharply and pushed her hand away. "No, thank you. I just need to go to the bank."

"Well, you can't go to the bank right now." And she laughed at me. It was meant to be a commiserating thing, like she understood getting caught out there with no money while other people waited

impatiently behind you. The way it echoed off my ears made my neck

tingle and my fists clench involuntarily.

Tyra handed the cashier her money. She gave Tyra the change

and shoved my bags in my direction. I snatched them up and pushed

Alexis out the door. Tyra was on my heels.

"If it'll make you feel better, you can pay me back."

But I'll tell you, what would have made me feel better was

pretending like I hadn't seen her. What would have made me feel

better was if my husband had never brought this woman to our house

three years ago.

It was easy to see why Malcolm liked Tyra Bettani. She was the

kind of person whose personality just jumped out at you from the start.

She wasn't shy about saying things that others might consider taboo in

mixed company. She was always smiling and in control and carefree.

She was an ob/gyn but she finished school two years ahead of

Malcolm because he'd taken time off after college to earn money for

medical school, a fact that she ribbed him about that night at dinner.

"That was such bullshit!" she'd said. "I came from the same

neighborhood you did, worked the same shit jobs you had and I still

managed to pay for school."

"Well, if my rich uncle had died and left me wads of money, I would have been able to do it too." Malcolm said this as he laughed into his glass of wine.

I twisted the stem of mine, wanting to laugh and feel easy about this conversation too. You see, I was dating Malcolm during the time he decided to hold off medical school. I'd encouraged him to do it.

"Now look at you," Tyra was smiling and saying. She leaned toward him and bumped him with her shoulder. He grinned. "You're married. You live in a house. In a nice neighborhood. Who'd have thought?"

"I'd have thought," he'd said. "I knew I was going to make it. I did." That's when he reached over and took my hand. That was the first time the whole night he acknowledged my presence.

That, too, seemed the time that Tyra noticed me. She looked over at me and smiled but it seemed painful. I think that our dislike of each other was instantaneous and unavoidable. For me, she was the girl that my husband always wanted but never got. To her, I was the girl that married the guy she didn't realize she wanted until it was too late.

I noticed her appraising my clothes. I was wearing a new dress but I was feeling self-conscious about it because I was about thirty pounds heavier then. That nasty stare made me want to cover myself and slink under the table. She seemed to be studying all the areas I was

embarrassed about and counting every out-of-place strand of my hair.

Then she smiled again but not too much, lest her face crack from the

effort.

So tell me more about Malcolm's little sweetheart, she'd said.

The question embarrassed me. I could tell by that look that she

was waiting for me to rattle off an impressive resume, something to

validate Malcolm's choice in a wife. But all I had were the facts and

they were very brief. I'm from New Brunswick. My family moved to

West Orange when I was eight. I went to high school there. I went to

college in North Carolina. I worked at Johnson & Johnson for about

two years and then I stopped working to take care of the house as

Malcolm wanted me to. That was all I had to say about me.

She guffawed and looked down at the table cloth for a moment

before turning back to Malcolm and saying, "Your wife is lovely."

"Yup," was all my husband said.

We finished dinner and Malcolm thought it would be a good

idea to do something fun. Like bowling, he said.

I sat in the back seat and watched while she fiddled with the

radio dial and he slapped her hand away. A song would come on that

reminded them of their childhood together and they would sing and

laugh over shared memories. Our wedding song came on and Malcolm looked back at me and grinned. But then Tyra squealed like a pig and said, "Remember when they played this at the prom and your date got mad because you danced with me?"

He quickly turned his attention back to her. He thought about what she said for a moment and then he too laughed.

"She was so fat!" Tyra laughed. "What was her name? Anne? Annette?"

"It was Amanda," he said. "And she was fat. She was really fat."

They laughed again. I couldn't stop hearing their laughter all night.

At the bowling alley, Tyra took the ball I was using. Every time she stepped up to bowl, she picked up my ball instead of the one she'd picked out for herself. She would hit a strike and dance her way back to Malcolm who gave her a high five and a little hug. I went to the bar and got a beer. I stayed there and nursed it. Every now and again I would glance over at them. But they just kept playing like I wasn't there. I finished my beer and drank three more. By the time I came back to them, I was very buzzed.

"Hey, where'd you go? Tyra had to bowl for you," Malcolm said when I came back.

"Yeah, sorry," she said. "I don't do too well playing for other people."

She'd gotten four gutter balls in a row. So far I had been playing with the highest score and now she'd knocked my nearly perfect game down to nothing. I was pissed and she just stood there grinning at me like an idiot. My face was so hot with rage that I felt like I would combust. I picked up my ball and threw it down the lane. "Now I have five gutter balls! Might as well not even play anymore."

"What's your problem?" Malcolm snapped. "It wasn't even your turn."

She reached out and touched his arm. I saw it for what it was. It was too intimate to be innocent, too knowing to be just between friends. That was when I knew from then on that I shouldn't ignore my instincts about her.

"It's okay, Malcolm," she said. "Now we've evened up the odds a bit, you know? Give us a chance to catch up to Kelly's winning streak."

Malcolm's face relaxed finally and he went up to bowl. But before he did, he smiled at her.

We didn't see her again until about seven or eight months later. Things between us had been a little tense at first but eventually returned to normal. It was around Christmas time and we were feeling more in the holiday spirit than ever. Malcolm was finally talking about kids and we were saving for this big vacation in the Caymans.

She called Malcolm as we were putting up the Christmas tree one evening. I could hear her voice through the phone, obviously distressed over something and looking for Malcolm to play her knight in shining armor. He was all too willing to fill the role. Twenty minutes later she was knocking on the door.

"Oh this looks lovely," she'd said of our decorations. She smiled up at me on the ladder. "How are you, Kelly?"

"Fine, thank you."

She took off her coat and tossed it onto a chair. "It's so cold out. I could use a nice warm cup of…something." She giggled.

Malcolm offered her tea and looked to me as though I was supposed to go and fetch it. I stared back at him until he got up and went into the kitchen himself. While he was gone, I finished putting up garland while pretending she wasn't there.

"So…you guys getting ready for the holidays?"

"It would appear so," I replied sarcastically.

"I remember when Malcolm and I used to have Christmas at my house when we were kids. Even when we got older, he still came over every year. Well, that is until he met you. Where did you meet

again?"

I remember thinking that was such a strange question to ask. I

turned to look at her. "He didn't tell you?"

She walked around touching things and running her finger

along surfaces. She rubbed her fingertips together and sniffed them.

"Not that I can recall."

"College."

"Oh right!" she said, slapping her forehead. "You were the nice

girl in his Anthropology class."

Malcolm came back in carrying her tea at that moment. I saw

her fingers slide over his as she took it from his hands. Her eyes

changed as she tilted the cup to her lips and sipped from it, never

looking away from him. "Did you put rum in this?"

"I know how you like it," he said. "Kelly drinks it the same

way." He pointed to my cup on the mantle.

"Really? A girl after my own heart."

"Sit down," Malcolm said to her. "Tell me what's going on."

So she starts telling him about this man she's been seeing for

the past eight months. She thought he was so great. Smart, successful

businessman with a Mercedes, an apartment in New York and a house

upstate. He was doing everything right, from fancy dinners to flowers, late night phone calls, ski trips in Vermont. He'd even met her parents.

And then, she said, he just stopped calling. One day, two days, a week.

Before she knew it, two and half weeks had gone by without so much

as an email.

So finally she gets in touch with him at his office and he tells

her that he's so sorry. He's been busy. Maybe it's not the right time for

him to see anyone seriously. He'd give her a call when things calmed

down. But he didn't know when that would be since he was so

swamped. A week later, she was coming out of a restaurant and there

he was "canoodling" with some blond bimbette in a mink coat. She

was wearing a rock the size of Mount Rushmore on her ring finger. His

cousin, he says to her. Like she was that stupid.

"I always pick losers," she sighed. "What's my problem?"

"Self-esteem," Malcolm answered. "That's always been your

problem."

I heard the couches moving behind me and I knew they were

moving closer together. I could almost hear their hands making

contact. I didn't turn around. I just kept hanging garland.

"For whatever reason, you don't seem to think you deserve

more than a loser. But you do. You're a terrific woman, Tyra."

Everything became too quiet for a moment and then I dropped

the tape. The sound jolted my heart back to life.

"We can finish that later, Kell," he said to me. "Come sit down."

But I couldn't sit down. I couldn't even turn myself around to face him. I would have done anything to not see their faces at that moment.

I began to feel nauseous. "I'm going to...I think I need to...lie down."

I ran upstairs and into the bathroom. I fell down on my knees and let my head rest on the seat. I heaved and coughed but nothing came up. Then I leaned back against the bathtub and stared up at the ceiling. What was wrong with me? I wondered. Why was I so consumed with dislike for this woman? Malcolm loved me. We'd been together for six and a half years. We owned a home together. We had a life with each other. He hadn't chosen to be with her. He could have but he didn't. He picked me and made me his wife.

Then I heard Tyra laughing. Malcolm laughed too, and it was the most delighted he'd sounded in God knows how long.

I leaned over the toilet and threw up my jealousy.

I was jealous of Tyra. I was jealous of her relationship with my husband. But mostly I was suspicious.

It was like Malcolm had been sick for a long time and suddenly someone had cured him. Before he was dragging himself out of bed and mumbling into his coffee. Now he moved around like springs were attached to his heels. He started speaking about work again with enthusiasm, he made love to me better and he started spending a lot of time hanging out with Tyra.

He would say that he was going out with a group of doctors. Just for drinks. Just to get some dinner and unwind a little. He never mentioned her as being part of that group but I knew she was. He came home and he smelled like her, but it was faint, and if you weren't looking for it, you'd never know it.

But that didn't last long. He started to become tense again. He was mumbling into his food and avoiding eye contact with me. I felt scared to approach him because he might explode. I never believed Malcolm would harm me in any way. But I can't deny that he frightened me at times.

One day he came home and slammed the door so hard that the house shook. He shouted my name like the place was on fire, and when I came out to see what was wrong, he slapped me on the cheek with an envelope.

"You want to tell me about this?" he said.

I was stunned from the slap. I mean, it didn't hurt but it was still a shock because he'd never done anything like that before. I stood there for a moment, trying to get my bearings again. He got impatient and shoved the letter into my palm and I saw that it was a bank statement. The letter had said that our account was overdrawn. We owed the bank a little over one thousand dollars.

I stood there while he stalked around me screaming about being responsible with the credit cards and not buying so much unnecessary shit like those new pokers for the fireplace that cost a pretty penny. A penny, he said, that we could have still had in the bank. Did I even think sometimes? I was going to charge us into the poor house! Then what would I do? Go running back to Mommy and Daddy, telling them how he fucked up? You know how much your father hates me anyway, he said. So how are we going to get this money back?

He didn't even give me a chance to explain before storming off. Then he wouldn't speak to me for the rest of the night. We ate dinner in silence. When he was done, he tossed his dishes in the sink and went down to the basement to run on the treadmill. That was for about an hour. He took a shower afterwards and went into the office where he sat and read until long after I'd gone to bed. The next morning, he was gone before I woke up.

Later that afternoon, as I was coming back from running a few errands, I saw Malcolm's car in the driveway. At that time, it wasn't uncommon for him to come home during the day to eat or shower. I was actually pleased that he was home because I wanted to smooth things over from the previous night and maybe make love before he went back in. But then I noticed Tyra Bettani's car sitting at the curb.

I pulled in behind Malcolm's car, got out and walked across the lawn. I glanced over at her car. She was still sitting inside. Malcolm was in there with her. My first impulse was to run over there and kick in the window. But I didn't do that. I just kept going into the house. I put my bags in the kitchen and went back to the front window. By that time, they were standing outside the car and Tyra looked like she'd been crying. Malcolm rubbed her arm and then leaned in and gave her a quick hug. Then she kissed his cheek and got back in her car. He watched her as she drove away.

He came into the kitchen while I was putting the groceries away. He waited for me to notice him but when I didn't speak he said, "That was Tyra. She just got some bad news."

Oh? I'd said. I didn't turn to look at him.

"Yeah," he said, moving closer to me. "Her fiancé just called off their wedding."

I hadn't even known she was engaged, I'd said. He had never mentioned it.

He shrugged and said, "I didn't think you'd care."

He was right about that. I didn't care. But I knew he did.

When he moved behind me and put his arms around my waist, I tensed. I had to force myself not to move away, not to let my feelings show in any part of me. Then he kissed the back of my neck and whispered, "I love you."

And I wanted to say it back because I did love my husband with all my heart. But this man was becoming less and less my husband every day. The Malcolm I fell in love with would never pull me close then push me away like this one did. My Malcolm didn't shout at me and he didn't hit me. I blamed Tyra Bettani for that. I blamed her for my insecurity, my helplessness. Malcolm adored her in a way that I couldn't stand. Maybe just as a friend, like he said. But it was adoration nonetheless and it killed me every time he talked to her or touched her or laughed with her. Whether they were sleeping together or not—which, at that point, I believed they weren't—didn't even matter. I knew Malcolm was entranced with her in a way he could never be with me. I was no Tyra Bettani.

But I was okay with that. I didn't want to be Tyra Bettani. Scratch the surface and she was a flake; a needy, insecure little girl who made a habit of taking things that didn't belong to her because it was easier to steal someone else's good thing than to work on her own. Why would I want to be like her?

As she stood there in front of me at the A&P parking lot, treating me like some welfare mom, I found the words I wanted to say to her.

"Why do you think you know my husband so well?" I asked her. "Who do you think you are telling me how to handle my own relationship?"

"I'm not trying to tell you how to handle your relationship, Kelly. I just—"

"That's funny, because it sure sounds like you are. I should make things 'easier' for him? If Malcolm had it any easier, he'd be comatose. Most nights he doesn't even come home while I'm cooking, cleaning, shopping, doing the finances and taking care of a five month old alone. Don't tell me I need to make it easier on him. Fuck him. And fuck you too."

And I walked away. I actually felt proud of myself for saying what I'd been wanting to say to her for years. Now we could wash away the pretense because she knew I didn't like her. I felt free again.

Yes, I was still upset and hurt over what Malcolm had done. But I was determined to hold it together.

Later that evening, I was sitting with Alexis while she was in her swing, slobbering over one of those infant cookies when Malcolm came in the door. She reached out her chubby arms to him and even managed a smile. It was so adorable and he barely acknowledged it. At that moment, he only had eyes for me.

He plopped down in his recliner and jiggled his keys in his hand. He always did that when he was trying to be calm about something that was really pissing him off. I didn't say anything. I waited for him to speak. "I heard you saw Tyra today."

I didn't know how much she'd told him so all I said was yes.

"She said you were rude to her."

She was rude to me first, I said.

"By helping you pay for the groceries? How is that rude?"

Because I didn't need her help, I told him. I could have gone to the bank.

"That was uncalled for, Kelly. I want you to apologize to her."

My eyes started burning and my chest ached. From the look on his face, I knew he was dead serious. But I still couldn't believe it. Why was he choosing her over me? How could he put this ring on my finger and treat me this way?

"You're joking, right?" I said.

"No, I'm not."

"Apologize for what?"

"For being rude. For acting like you don't have any manners."

I shook my head. "I'm not apologizing to her."

"If you were a real woman, you'd call her up and apologize."

I couldn't hear anymore. It was just too insane to listen to anymore. Was I in a dream or something?

I used the arm of the sofa to balance myself. Then I bent and picked up Alexis.

"I need to wash her up and get her ready for bed. You can see yourself out."

"Kelly!"

I didn't come back downstairs until I was sure that he was gone. Then I started looking for a mess to clean. I wanted to do something that I had to think about so I wouldn't think about him. So I started baking cookies. While I was doing that, the phone rang. I didn't want to answer because I thought it might be Malcolm or Tyra. I was relieved to hear my best friend's voice.

Sara started talking right away about something. I kept spooning mounds of dough onto the cookie sheets, barely listening to her. I couldn't take my mind away from what I was doing or

everything would unravel.

"Kelly?"

"Uh huh."

"You're not listening."

"Oh."

"Do you want me to call you back?"

"Maybe."

"Kelly!"

"What?!" I dropped my spoon on the counter and touched my

forehead. I was sweating.

"What is wrong with you?" she asked. "Have you been

listening to a thing I said?"

"No. I'm sorry. Things are just crazy here." I fell into a chair.

"Malcolm left."

"What? What do you mean he left?"

I started to cry. It was the first time since the night before I'd

even let myself go there. I sobbed into the phone and clutched my

stomach. I felt like I was in physical pain.

"He left me," I sobbed. "He came home and said he wanted to

live somewhere else for a while and then he packed his stuff and she

called him and he left to go to dinner with her!"

"Was it Tyra?"

"Yes."

"Oh, Kelly. I'm sorry."

I sat there and cried for half an hour. Sara tried to comfort me as best she could over the telephone. I felt like I'd been ripped apart. I didn't even try to delude myself with the notion that this was temporary. Everything in my body told me that my marriage was over. Whether it was Tyra Bettani or the inevitable, I couldn't be sure.

Eventually Sara had to go but she told me she would stop by first thing tomorrow to check on me. When I hung up the phone, I just stood there. I don't know how long I was there. Could have been hours. I was just so dead inside all of a sudden. But maybe that's inaccurate. Maybe it wasn't so sudden at all. Maybe it had been happening for years and I just failed to see it. At any rate, I had to figure out what to do next.

I called Malcolm's mother later that evening. It might have been the night after. I'm not really sure. I called her just because I wanted to know if he'd told his family. I could tell by her voice that he had.

She was very cold on the phone. "Oh, hello. How are you?" she said.

"Fine," I had said. "I wanted to tell you about something cute Alexis did the other day."

I made up some story about the baby trying to say her name, Agnes, and then I told her I had to go because I left something in the oven. I figured that if Malcolm's mom knew, then he'd been lying when he told me why he was going. It hadn't been sleep at all. But then again, I always knew that.

Being one of those women, a left woman, dumped, discarded, abandoned, pissed me off. I never wanted to be like that. I've seen so many other women try and fail at relationships, always wanting to know what they did wrong. You just have to know how to handle yourself. I always believed that I could do it right. There was never a doubt in my mind. I was going to make sure that my man was the perfect man and that he would be strong enough to resist temptations. He would take our vows as seriously as I did till the day one of us died. I guess Malcolm almost made it.

I didn't hear from him for a while. Life went on as usual for me and the baby. Like I said before, Malcolm was hardly ever home so it was easy to treat this thing like the norm.

There's this bar and grill on Montgomery Street called Kippy's. I was meeting a gentleman there for a dinner date. He had delivered a package for Malcolm one day and we started talking. It was nice, you know? Alexis is an adorable baby but she's not very good company for an adult. At that time it had been about five or six months since Malcolm left. I don't think I was really interested in this guy more than I just wanted to go out and fuck someone. That's what they say you should do to get over someone. Just slide beneath the next contestant.

I didn't have sex with him though. There was nothing but a kiss on the cheek. But I would have invited him in except that Tyra Bettani came to the door as we were saying good night.

I know you're probably thinking that she always pops up at inopportune times. Well, you're right about that. I couldn't turn away for a second without turning back and finding her there. She always looked at me so innocently, like she could feel my hostility and she honestly didn't know where it came from.

"Hi, Kelly," she said. She glanced at my date and smiled a little. "Can I talk to you please?"

I didn't try to hide my irritation with her. I said, "Actually, I don't want to talk to you. And I'm busy as you can see."

"Please," she said, grabbing my sleeve. "It's important."

"It's okay," my date said. "I'll call you later."

I barely noticed when he walked off. I was staring down at her hand clutching my coat. I pulled my arm back and glared at her. I wanted my look to tell her everything I was too much of a lady to say. I couldn't stand this woman and I would have ripped her limb from limb if it weren't for my daughter. I just couldn't risk Malcolm taking her away from me because, at the time, she was all I had left.

"What do you want?"

She sighed and chewed on her bottom lip, like whatever she had to say was killing her to admit. "Well, I didn't want to be the one to have to do this. I told Malcolm he should come to you."

My blood got cold at that moment. I was so taut that I could have snapped if I moved. I think she knew that. I think she was relishing my anxiety.

"Malcolm and I are seeing each other."

It'd been exactly what I knew she would say. She was waiting for me to react appropriately. You know, tears and anger and screams. I wouldn't give either of them the satisfaction. Like I said before, she wasn't really telling me anything I didn't already know. Only difference now was that the game had changed. Malcolm was sending her in to do his dirty work. That was typical of him. He was about three inches short of being a man, if you know what I mean.

"Did you hear what I said?" she asked.

Yes, I said. Loud and clear.

"Are you angry?"

"Why should I be?" I crossed my arms and assumed a bored stance.

"Well," she said, "he is still your husband. He took vows with you."

Vows which stopped mattering the second he left our home. I don't care anymore, I told her.

"Oh," she said.

Then she looked up at me and I knew it was coming. I could hear it like a train approaching and I was standing in the center of the tracks.

"I'm pregnant. And it's Malcolm's."

"So what you're saying, Miss Jacoby--"

"Jacoby is my maiden name, Officer. Please call me Stewart."

The detectives exchanged looks. Detective Jacks sat down at the table and laced his fingers together. The light reflected off his glasses as he stared at her.

Beads of sweat were sliding down the bulbous, ruddy face of Detective Roberts. "Excuse me, *Mrs. Stewart.*"

"Thank you," she smiled courteously.

Jacks cleared his throat. "So what you're telling us is that Ms. Bettani came to you and told you that your husband was cheating with her and that she was now pregnant?"

"That's correct."

"What time would you say it was when Ms. Bettani left?"

She thought about it for a moment. "I'd say it was close to 11 or so."

"And do you remember how long the two of you spoke before she left?"

"It wasn't long," she said. "Only about six or seven minutes. I didn't even invite her in. After her admission, I just wanted to get as far away from her as I could."

"So you went inside the house?"

"Yes."

"Did you do anything?"

Her eyes narrowed as she tried to recall. "I think I took off my shoes and left them by the stairs and then I went straight upstairs and undressed. I read for a while and then I went to sleep."

"Okay," he said. He clicked his pen and scribbled something on the yellow notepad in front of him. "What did you read?"

"Excuse me?"

He glanced up at her. "What was the name of the book?"

"Oh, it wasn't a book." She grinned and laughed a little. "Sorry, I guess I spaced out for a second."

"Magazine then?"

"No, actually, it was a pamphlet that I keep in my nightstand drawer. See, I joined this group down at the YWCA for divorced women. It's not really religious but we have literature to remind us to be thankful for God's blessings and what not."

"Where was your daughter?" Roberts asked.

"With my mother."

Jacks stopped writing and flipped back a few pages. "Your mother who lives in Rhode Island? How can you have taken your baby to Rhode Island in one evening and returned with enough time to go on your date?"

She stared at them blankly. "My mother was visiting at the time. She was staying at the Ramada."

"We checked on that," the white cop said, pushing himself off the wall with his elbow. "There was no reservation for a Mrs. Jacoby. None of the staff remember seeing an older woman with a baby at all during the time your mother was supposed to be there." He laid his palms on the table and leaned close to her. "So why don't you tell us where the baby was."

"Oh!" she exclaimed. "You're absolutely right. I'm so silly. Alexis was with Sara."

"Sara Mezzano?"

"Yes, Detectives."

Jacks wrote something else. "Mrs. Stewart, can you recall what you were doing when you received a call that your husband had been killed?"

"Absolutely," she stated firmly. "I was packing up the rest of his things."

"Malcolm's things?" Roberts asked.

"Yes."

"Why were you doing that?"

"Well, I figured it was about time to do it. He'd obviously moved on. There was no sense in keeping that stuff out. All it would do was remind me that my husband had left me."

"What did you do with his belongings?"

"I put them on the curb for trash pick up the next morning."

The white cop groaned and yanked a chair away from the table. "I'd like to just change the line of questioning here for a minute."

He squeezed his frame into the chair. "Now," he said. "You're telling me—us—that this woman came to you and confirmed your suspicion that she had been sleeping with your husband and all you did was go to your room and read a pamphlet?"

She stared at him without blinking. "Yes."

"You expect us to believe that."

"Yes."

"Why?"

"Because it's the truth."

"No offense, but I don't believe a word of this."

"Roberts," the other officer said. He sighed retiringly. "Mrs. Stewart, can you excuse us for a moment?"

"Absolutely, Detective."

He followed Roberts out into the hallway and closed the door. Roberts turned to him, his meaty fists propped on his hips. "She's cunning."

"Yeah, but not very smart."

"I mean, she just has an answer for everything," he said. "Why are we even wasting our time? We know she did this."

"We don't have enough evidence to support that."

"Aw, come on! She's scamming us. Plain and simple."

"Yeah, I know it," Detective Jacks said. "Just like you know it and everybody else knows it. But the only way we're going to get her is to catch her in her lies. And believe me, buddy, she's spun a web so intricate, she's liable to get stuck somewhere."

Roberts sighed and pulled his hand down his face. "Shall we go in and let her continue?"

"After you."

She was staring at the door when they came back inside. She smiled and folded her hands on the table. "I really need to go soon. I have to get my daughter."

"We'll be done soon," Roberts said.

"Well, no disrespect officer," she said, "but you said that three hours ago."

Jacks stared at her. "We'll be done soon."

"Now," Roberts said, dropping his big frame back into the chair. "Tell us again what happened when Ms. Bettani came to your house."

"She told me she was sleeping with my husband and that she was pregnant."

"And what'd you do?"

"I let her say what she came to say and then I went inside."

"You didn't respond to her?"

"Beyond telling her that I didn't care, no. I don't like confrontation and as I told you earlier, I don't handle myself well in situations like that."

"When was the last time you saw Tyra Bettani?"

She thought about it for a moment. "About two months later."

Both detectives looked at one another. "So that night she came to your house wasn't the last time she saw you?"

"Yes," she said. "It was the last time she saw me. But it wasn't the last time I saw her."

"What does that mean, Miss Jacoby?" Jacks asked.

"It means that I saw her at my doctor's office two months later."

Roberts snorted. "So now you have the same doctor? I tell you, for two women who hate each other, you sure keep finding ways to entangle your lives with the other."

"Trust me, officer," Kelly said. "I think the same thing."

"Did you speak?"

"She didn't see me. I had just gotten there as she was leaving."

"Mrs. Stewart, are you aware that Tyra Bettani has been reported missing by her family and coworkers? They say she hasn't come to work in almost a month. That would place her disappearance around the time that Malcolm was killed. What do you have to say about that?"

"She's pregnant," Kelly said. "Maybe she took an early maternity leave. I don't know what happened to her and I couldn't care less."

"You're cold."

"No. It's just a little chilly in here, that's all."

"That's not what I meant," Roberts said. "I meant you're callous, calculating and cunning. You're pissed off that your husband abandoned you so you got revenge."

"No, I didn't," she said calmly. "Believe me, I wish I had gotten revenge. I was pissed but not enough to hurt anyone."

"You were pissed all right," he said. "Pissed enough to stalk your husband for weeks and sneak up behind him like a rat in an alley and blow his brains all over the place?"

"No."

"How 'bout pissed enough to follow his pregnant girlfriend to her apartment and bludgeon her to death before hiding the body?"

"You are sick," Kelly fairly spat.

"No, Mrs. Stewart. You're the sick one here and we're going to prove that. When we find the body of Tyra Bettani it's all going to come down on you."

"That's an inaccurate conclusion," she said, becoming exasperated. "Honestly, this is like watching a cop drama on television."

"I assure you there is nothing fake about this situation," Jacks said.

She fixed a hard stare on him. "My husband walked out on me for this woman. My daughter no longer has a father. I wouldn't even dare to suggest that this is fake."

"Why were you at the doctor?"

She groaned and rolled her eyes. "Why wouldn't I go to the doctor? I sure hope you two don't get paid a lot because you really don't know what you're doing."

"Why don't you let us be the judge of that?" Jacks said.

"Well, I'd like to, sir, but I resent ineptitude, especially when it wastes my time."

Roberts slapped his mitt over a folder at the end of the table. He yanked it up and tossed photo after photo onto the table in front of her. "See these? See what you did to the man who is the father of your child?"

Kelly turned away and swallowed her revulsion. "I don't want to see those."

"Why not?" he demanded. "You saw it when you did it. What's so different now?"

He collected the photos and slipped them back in the folder. Then he went over to Jacks and whispered something before leaving the room.

Jacks sat down in front of her and folded his hands together. They stared at each other for a moment before Jacks said, "What were you doing at the doctor's office?"

I was dating again. I never thought I would have to be back out there and suddenly I was thrust into the whole awkward, clumsy scene again. I hadn't dated much in college, just a few guys here and there. I'd certainly never been promiscuous. I wasn't raised that way. In all the time since Malcolm left, I'd only had the one date with the delivery guy and that went nowhere. I was sick of feeling alone, so I went for it.

Sara and I were going to bars and comedy clubs, places where we thought we could meet halfway decent guys. The goal, she said, was not to meet the next husband but the next orgasm. Let loose and have fun. So I did. I danced and laughed and chatted with faceless men. Then I met Thomas.

Thomas was a computer technician. He mostly worked with big corporations and spent a lot of time traveling around to different cities. On occasion, he would take a smaller job and that's how he came

to be in my office that day.

With Malcolm off shacking up with Tyra, I had to make my

own way. Bills had to be paid and Alexis had to go to daycare. So I

took a job as an analyst. Thomas was sweet and friendly, flirting with

me as he worked at the terminal directly across from my desk. I didn't

want to go out with him but he was so persistent that I begrudgingly

accepted.

We went on three dates before we had sex. It was great, mostly

because it felt like vindication. When I came, I imagined that Malcolm

was watching and seething with jealousy. It made it that much better.

Unfortunately, Thomas was only as nice as he needed to be to

get into my panties. After that night, he stopped calling. He never came

back to our office to finish linking our networks but he did manage to

leave me with an uncomfortable itch and terrible burning when I

urinated. Needless to say I was embarrassed. Technically, I was still

married and here I was with an STD. I waited for about a week before I

finally made the appointment to see my doctor.

When I arrived, I saw her coming out of the office. She'd gotten

much bigger since I'd last seen her. Malcolm wasn't with her. My guess

was that he was at the hospital. Something about her was different. All

the glitz and glitter that used to surround her was gone. Her hair was pulled back into a messy ponytail, she was wearing old, grungy jeans,

ratty sneakers and a faded college T-shirt. As she walked toward her

car, she kept her head down and when she got in, she sat behind the

wheel for a moment before pulling away.

When I got in to see Dr. Fisher, I made up some story about

seeing my old high school classmate—Tyra—on her way out but I

hadn't had a chance to talk to her before she pulled away. So she was

pregnant, huh? How far along is she? She looked sad. Is everything

okay?

Of course, Dr. Fisher told me nothing. He gave me medication

for my disease and some condoms, scolding me about safe sex practices

like I was some rambunctious teenager. I took them and I smiled but as

soon as I got outside, I tossed them in the trash. I wouldn't need them

because I was giving up sex indefinitely. I'd learned my lesson.

The only person I told about seeing Tyra was Sara. She and I

actually had a good laugh over it. Whatever jealousy I had harbored

toward Tyra before had all but dissipated. Now she was me, the person

she mocked and laughed at. When I saw her and the look on her face,

the pure dread and bone-deep sadness that made her pause right

where she was, I felt like I really knew her for the first time. That had

been me for such a long time. It's funny how I didn't even remember that, at one point, I had been quite lovely, I had been fashionable, I had

been smart and educated.

It seemed that just as it was all coming back to me, it was all

going away from her. Did I sympathize? A little. But this is the point

I'm trying to make. As much as I loved my husband, I also knew how

draining our relationship had been. Malcolm was too insecure to want

a woman like Tyra to *stay* a woman like Tyra. I'll bet the reason she

stopped going to work was because he told her to. He couldn't have his

wife bringing in more money than him. How would that make him

look? See, for Malcolm, being a husband and a father was more an

insignia of his pride. Those were all the things a successful man was

supposed to have. And he was hell-bent on proving himself to be just

that.

It was ironic, actually, how free I felt in spite of my pain.

Things were vastly different for Alexis and me, but we have learned to

adjust. Truth to be told, I didn't even miss him after a while. And that

was a good thing. As all those emotions left me, they took my anger

too. I had let it go and managed to stay afloat. That is until he took my

daughter.

It was Alexis's birthday. I'd made special plans to leave work

early that day and take her to the park. Before he left, Malcolm and I

had talked about having a huge celebration for her 1st birthday but I'd pretty much fallen out of the good graces of everyone we knew. Sara is the only friend I have here. Everyone else is back in Rhode Island.

My mom called me as I was on the way there. I was trying to balance the phone under my ear and the wheel with half my attention and I swerved and hit another car in the opposite direction. The damage wasn't bad at all but this woman was freaking out at me. She was screaming and threatening to sue. The police arrived and we had to go through that whole mess before they let either of us go. By that time it was nearly six thirty and my daughter was still at school.

The parking lot was empty except one car. I recognized it as the head teacher's car. I rushed inside, knowing that I would be reprimanded for arriving so late when the school closes at five-thirty. But Mrs. Floyd — the teacher — was locking up just as I approached the front door and she didn't have Alexis.

"Where's Alexis?" I asked, half panicked.

"Your husband came and got her," she said huffily. "And we'd appreciate if you'd call the next time you're going to be late. We have husbands and children of our own to get home to."

"I'm sorry," I said. "I was in an accident. Where did my husband take her? He's not allowed to take her. I didn't give permission for that."

Mrs. Floyd became very insulted. "I'm well aware of who you did and did not give permission to retrieve your daughter. However, Mr. Stewart's name *was* on the contact sheet. Perhaps you don't remember filling that part out."

With that she stormed away.

I was hysterical. For a moment, I completely forgot where I was and what I was doing there. How could Malcolm do that? I thought. Why would he take her and not even call me? That's when I realized that this was Malcolm flexing his muscle. This was his way of showing me that he still had some control over me and our daughter was living proof of that.

I called his cell phone and of course, he did not answer. I left a message on his voice mail telling him that if he did not return my daughter to me within the next seven hours, there was going to be hell to pay. I was shaking on the drive home and stopped at a liquor store to buy a little something to douse the inflammation of nerves. With every hour that passed, I paced and waited. I picked up the phone so many times to call the police I lost count. Sara tried to calm me down, reminding me that Malcolm wasn't callous enough to hurt Alexis. He was just being a dick.

But I wasn't worried about him hurting Alexis. Not once was this ever about her. Not even his taking her was about her. It was a way to get at me for whatever reason. I didn't see why he felt the need

to create some dramatic scene with it, but most things that Malcolm did

hardly made any sense to me.

Finally, with less than thirty minutes remaining in the seven

hours I'd given him, the doorbell rings and Malcolm is standing there

with Alexis. She was asleep, draped over his shoulder like a rag doll.

Her face was blue and sticky from cotton candy, her fingernails were

jammed with chocolate. He passed her off to me and I immediately

took her to her bedroom to wash her up and place in her crib. The relief

I felt was indescribable. All I wanted to do was smother her with hugs

and kisses. But instead I just let her sleep and went back to the living

room for another drink.

Malcolm was still there. He was standing by the mantle,

staring at pictures of memories he'd missed. He picked up one photo

and said, "I want to keep this."

"Where did you take her?" I demanded.

"It's her birthday," he said. "I took her to the amusement

park."

"Without asking me? Without even telling me what you were

going to do? How could you do that? I was worried sick!"

He smiled this incredibly nasty smile—evidently, he'd picked that up from Tyra—and said, "When would you have time to worry while you're sleeping around town?"

I wanted nothing more than to slap him across his arrogant, self-righteous face. But Malcolm wasn't above hitting back and as strong as I may have felt, ultimately I knew that he was still stronger.

"That's none of your business," I said.

"Technically, you're still my wife and what I say goes."

"Technically, you left me and fucked that bitch Tyra Bettani and got her pregnant. You don't have any say here, Malcolm. So why don't you get the hell out? And by the way, if you ever remove my daughter from school again without *my* permission, I'll have you arrested so fast you'll—"

I didn't get to finish before he reached out with lightning speed and clutched a handful of my hair in his fist. He twisted and pulled until I cried out and tears popped in my eyes. "You'll what?" he whispered in my ear. "Try it, bitch. Try it and see what I'll do to you."

He smashed his lips over mine, jamming his tongue between my lips. His free hand unbuttoned my blouse and squeezed my breast so hard I screamed. He threw me down on the couch…sorry…

Give me a second…

He threw me down on the couch and pushed my skirt up. He scratched my inner thigh with his watch. I tried to get away but he was so heavy on top of me. Then he ripped my panties and tried to shove his fingers inside me...can we take a break for a minute?

"Sure," Jacks said. "Would you like some water or soda?"

"Yes, please," Kelly said, clutching her clammy fingers together.

Jacks stuck his head out the door and called for someone to bring him a soda. He sat the can in front of her and took his seat again.

"You're saying that Mr. Stewart raped you?"

"No," she said. "He didn't. It was like a miracle from God because the phone rang and the baby cried at the same time. I guess he came back to his senses because he got off me and he left."

"Who was on the phone?"

"A man that I'd made a date with earlier in the week. He was just calling to make sure we were still on for that Saturday. I started to cry. He offered to come over but I told him no and I hung up to go see about Alexis."

"Did Ms. Bettani ever find out about your husband's attack?"

Kelly shrugged. "I don't know. I told you I didn't see her again after that day at Dr. Fisher's office."

Jacks wrote something on his pad. "Where were you on the day of your husband's murder?"

I don't know where I was on the exact day. I know where I was when I heard about it.

The mail had come earlier than usual that Saturday. I went out to get it and found a letter for Malcolm in there. He'd stopped most of his mail from coming here but every now and again an odd piece would find its way back to the house. I usually shredded them no matter how important they seemed and if he asked me about them in his infrequent phone calls, I feigned ignorance. But that day, I didn't just toss it because I noticed the return address was from my doctor. I couldn't imagine what my doctor would be sending a letter to Malcolm about so I opened it.

It was a bill for Tyra's last visit. Somehow she had been able to use his insurance to cover them. There was an outstanding balance and a current balance that totaled over a thousand dollars. Malcolm and I still had joint accounts and the only place he could be getting his money was from one of them. I immediately called the bank and sure enough, he'd cleaned us out. Everything was gone. Not one cent was left. I almost lost it. I could have killed him for not thinking of Alexis. You always hear these stories of how men leave their wives and kids and cut them off completely but I never thought Malcolm would do that. I never imagined that he'd leave us out to dry that way.

That was when I started packing up his stuff. Everything that was left was leaving. I even threw out our wedding photos and albums. I had no use for them and I certainly didn't want them around to remind me of what I falsely presumed to be real love, a strong bond and commitment. In retrospect, I should have saved a few things for Alexis but if I had known that someone would kill Malcolm, I certainly wouldn't have gotten rid of them.

I remember that the phone was ringing when I came back in from sitting the trash on the curb. I ran to answer it but whoever it was had already hung up. I went about my normal Saturday activities; cleaning, doing the laundry, sorting and paying the bills (I was smart enough to keep a private checking account as well). The phone rang again but it stopped after two rings. Then it rang again and stopped. I used the return call service and was surprised to hear the operator repeating Malcolm's cell phone number. I called it back. A woman answered who I assumed to be Tyra.

"Why have you been calling my house?" I demanded, not waiting for her to address herself.

"Who is this?" the woman's voice asked.

"Don't play dumb, Tyra. You know who it is."

"No," the woman said, "I'm afraid I don't. I don't know how to use this darn thing and I was trying to call someone. This is Mrs. Stewart."

"Oh," I said, confused. "Did I dial the wrong number? I was trying to reach Malcolm's cell."

There was pause. Then a soft sob. "This is Malcolm's phone. Is this Kelly?"

"Yes, Agnes, it's me," I said. "What's the matter?"

That's when she told me. She burst into tears and cried, "Someone killed my Malcolm! Someone killed my baby boy!"

I must have dropped the phone because I don't remember hearing her say anything else. I felt sick. I fell to the floor and just sat there listening to Agnes sob. The house was still otherwise. I felt like I was waking up from a really bad dream only to realize that it really wasn't a dream at all. Images of a brutal attack flipped through my brain like frames from a motion picture. Had they shot him, beaten him, stabbed him? Who would do such a thing?

My mother drove from Rhode Island to be with me and Alexis. A bunch of funeral homes called to solicit my business but I told them to call Malcolm's mother. I wanted no part of the plans. No one else had called except Sara. I don't doubt that if I hadn't called his cell phone that day, Mrs. Stewart would have "conveniently" forgotten to

tell me about it. I would have had to read it in the papers like a
common stranger. I knew that we were estranged and I expected no
special treatment, but he was still my husband.

The funeral was a showy affair. Malcolm's fellow residents at
the hospital were given front row seats. I, his wife, and his baby
daughter were relegated to the back of the room. Even if Malcolm were
alive, I'm sure he'd have it no other way.

At one point during the lengthy service, a man came up to me
with a bouquet of white tulips. "I don't know if you remember me," he
said. "I met you years ago when Malcolm was an intern."

I didn't remember him but I smiled anyway and accepted his
tulips. He smiled at Alexis, who I was balancing on my hip, and
chucked her under the chin. "Wow, she's beautiful. She looks like
you."

"Thank you." Someone bumped me hard from behind and
kept going. "Jesus."

"Why don't we move out of the herd's way," he said.

We moved away from the huddles of loudly conversing
groups to a quiet corner beside a table lined with food.

"I just wanted to say that I'm sorry for what happened," he
leaned close to say.

"Me too," I said ruefully. "I wish we knew who was responsible."

"No," he said, a little embarrassed, I think. "I meant about Malcolm and Dr. Bettani. I warned her not to get involved with him because of his track record but she kept saying she knew him very well."

"Track record?"

He paused and stared at me. "Shit. You didn't know. I'm sorry...I just assumed that was why you were separating. When Malcolm told me...fuck! I'm sorry. I have to go."

"Wait a minute," I said, pulling him back. "Don't walk away. Tell me what you mean."

He looked trapped and desperate to get away from me but I made him stay and tell me everything he knew. We found two empty seats and he took a deep breath before spilling out everything he knew.

"Malcolm," he said, "was always popular with the female interns. Here he was, this big handsome black doctor. It really got them going, you know? At first he brushed off the attention to concentrate on work. But then when he started his residency, I noticed that he was spending a lot of time with one of the new interns. This really dopey girl who was too eager to learn. He was annoyed by her at first but after a while it was always just the two of them.

"I guess when he was done with her, he moved on. There were a bunch of them, most of them interns. Once or twice I saw him meeting with women outside the hospital. Then Dr. Bettani came."

"Did you know she was pregnant?" I asked him.

He nodded. "You hear whispers in the corridors. They'd fight in front of everyone. It was hard not to notice. She stopped coming to work at the beginning of her third trimester."

It was then that I noticed Tyra was not there. I hadn't seen her at all the whole day. The man excused himself when my mother came over. She took Alexis and said, "Why don't you go home and lie down? You look exhausted."

"I can't," I told her. "Alexis just had a nap an hour ago. She's not going to want to sleep."

"I'll take care of her. Go home. We'll join you in a little while."

I should have gone home. I know it. And you're going to think all the wrong things when I tell you this.

I found Malcolm's mother and asked her about Tyra. She was reluctant to tell me anything and I wondered how much she really knew, or had known, since the beginning. But I couldn't risk her making a big scene so I pretended to be concerned about all this and Tyra's delicate condition. The only thing Agnes told me was that a

week or so before his death, Malcolm said that Tyra was on bed rest
until she delivered the baby.

You probably already know that I saw her records; that I paid
the receptionist at Dr. Fisher's office to let me take a peek at them. It's
not so hard to spot someone with questionable morals. Nothing in
Tyra's chart suggested that she needed to be on bed rest. She was
healthy, the baby was fine and at a normal weight. Everything was
perfect for the perfect life that she'd stolen from me. The only notation
Dr. Fisher made was possible depression.

That's where I got her address too. I went there. I lied about
being a cousin in town for the weekend and managed to get past the
security desk. They even escorted me upstairs. I knocked but she didn't
answer. I must have stood outside her door for twenty minutes or so. I
don't know what made me turn the knob. But the door was already
opened. I didn't break into her apartment.

There was nothing unusual except the stillness. Everything
was covered in thick gray-brown dust. She'd left a half-eaten banana
on the table that had turned oily black and attracted flies. One window
stood open in the living room. I don't remember touching anything
except the doorknob and her purse, which was still sitting on the bed. I
thought it was odd that she wasn't there and yet her purse was. But

maybe she switched purses and just forgot to transfer some of the stuff to the other one.

Her apartment wasn't as chic as I imagined it would be. It was actually pretty simple. Lots of hand-me-down furniture and antiquey looking items here and there. The only thing ultra-modern was the computer and fax machine on a worn desk in front of the bedroom windows. Her sofa was threadbare on the arms and stained on the cushions. The television was old, the remote control had lost the backing to hold in the batteries. Her carpet was rough and matted and this really unattractive dark burgundy. Can you imagine a doctor living in this ritzy two thousand-dollar a month apartment with cheap furniture?

I stopped at a fast food place before going home, just to give myself an alibi in case my mother was already there with the baby. Hers and Sara's cars were parked along the curb in front of the house.

"Where have you been?" my mother asked. Sara was on the floor playing the Alexis.

"I was hungry," I said. "I didn't get anything to eat at the service."

"Hi," Sara said. "I just wanted to make sure you were okay."

"I'm fine. I'm going to go upstairs to lie down."

I left them with the bag of food and went straight upstairs to shower and change. The whole thing was becoming very lurid. There were so many question marks and unexplained things. I wasn't concerned for Tyra but the fact that she was inexplicably gone worried me.

Roberts came back into the room. Officer Jacks motioned him into a chair. "Still not ready to confess, Mrs. Stewart?"

Kelly sighed wearily. "I've told you again and again. I don't have anything to confess to. I didn't kill my husband and I had nothing to do with Tyra's disappearance. For all any of us know, *she* could have killed Malcolm and flown to Tahiti to have their love child."

"That's an awfully sensational story," Roberts grinned. "You're pretty good at fabricating tales, aren't you?"

"No," she said firmly. "Now I've been really nice so far by not requesting my lawyer. If you keep baiting me, I'll do just that."

Roberts leaned back in his chair but never let his cold stare waver from her face.

"I think we're done for now, Mrs. Stewart," Jacks said.

The door opened and a woman came in to hand Roberts a file. He flipped through it and read. "Just one minute, Detective Jacks. I have some more questions."

Kelly groaned and said, "Please, Officer. I really need to get my baby and I'm tired of answering the same questions again and again."

"Just sit tight," Roberts said. He closed the file and folded his hands before him. "Tell me about Sara Mezzano."

"What's to tell? She's my best friend."

"For how long?"

"We met in college. We weren't really that close then. She was just someone I knew. When I came back to Pennsylvania from Rhode Island to marry Malcolm, she and I struck up a friendship."

"Aren't you forgetting something about Ms. Mezzano that could be relevant to this case?"

Kelly shook her head, confused. "No."

Roberts passed the folder over to Jacks. "So, you've conveniently forgotten that Malcolm was dating Ms. Mezzano when he met you? And that he had been cheating on Ms. Mezzano for over a year before she found out?"

"That wasn't me," she said. "That was another girl. And Sara never said anything about dating Malcolm in college."

"Did he?"

"No," Kelly said. "He liked Sara. He didn't treat her like an ex-girlfriend. In fact, I remember the day I introduced them. They acted like they didn't know each other."

"Acted is right," Roberts said. "They know each other very well. They have two children together."

Kelly became very still. Her eyes flashed back and forth from Jacks to Roberts. "No."

"Yes," Roberts said. He pulled the folder back. "One minor male youth, Tobias Mezzano, age 9. One minor female youth, Elizabeth Mezzano, age 6."

"Those are her brother's kids. Sara doesn't have any children. She can't. She had uterine cancer in high school and had a hysterectomy."

"Is that what she told you?" Roberts laughed. "A hysterectomy in high school? It's funny how none of her medical records report the procedure. Two happy, healthy kids, they do report."

"That's no proof that they're Malcolm's. Sara dated a lot. They could be anyone's kids."

Jacks handed her a piece of paper. "DNA testing was done on both children two years ago when Ms. Mezzano tried to sue for child support. They are his children."

"And I think you knew that," Roberts said.

"You're full of shit," Kelly hissed. "And I'm not going to sit here and listen to-"

"You'll sit there and listen to whatever the hell I tell you to!" he snapped. "I say you *did* know Sara Mezzano was screwing your husband back in college! I say you knew about *all* the other women he was seeing. I say you fucking flipped when you found out about the kids and I say you killed your husband! Then, knowing that Tyra Bettani could come between you and Malcolm's estate, you killed her too!"

Kelly shook her head, tears making pale coppery tracks down her cheeks. "I didn't know about Sara. I didn't know she lied to me."

"You're the liar here," Roberts said. "You knew damn well what was going on. All of this is just a smoke screen."

"Just tell us how you did it, Kelly," Jacks said. "Tell us what lead to the argument and how you and Sara planned this whole thing."

There was no argument. When you hate somebody as much as I hated Malcolm, you don't need anything in particular to trigger the act. All you really need is a bunch of lucky coincidences and enough nerve to go through with it.

Sara was the nerve. I didn't want to do it myself. I wanted him dead, but I didn't want the blood on my hands. That day when he told me I didn't have any manners and that I wasn't a *real* woman like Tyra, I was so fucking angry. I could have torn him apart with my bare hands. Sara didn't call me. I called her and I told her what had just happened. She was just as livid as I was, as though he'd said it to her. Maybe, in the distant past, he had. Maybe he'd said those exact words to her about me.

Did I know they had dated? Yes. But not at first. Not for a long time, actually. It came out during a girls' night that she and I had. We were drinking and talking and sharing stories about old boyfriends and she slipped. We sobered right up after that and she told me everything. Well, everything except that she knew that I was the girl Malcolm had cheated on her with. I was angry. I should have been angry and I don't feel bad for that. But after a while, I...I just had no other friends. And so I forgave her. And she assured me that she had no current interest in him.

That night on the phone was when Sara said it. She said that we should just kill him. It would make both of our lives easier.

"Why yours?" I had asked.

"Because then I don't have to listen to you bitch about him all the time."

We laughed. "I just can't believe he would do this to me, Sara."

"I know, sweetie. Malcolm's a dog. Always has been. Tyra Bettani will learn that sooner or later."

"Well, she deserves whatever she gets," I said.

"And Malcolm will too."

"Yeah. Well, I guess we'll have to wait until he's burning in hell someday. By then I probably won't even care."

She was quiet for a moment. Then, "We don't have to wait that long, Kelly."

"Does he have something terminal I don't know about?" I asked.

"A bullet in his back is pretty terminal, I'd say."

"Sara..."

"I'm serious. Why *don't* we just kill him? It'll be so easy."

"Are you fucking crazy?" I asked. "I'm not going to do that."

"Then I'll do it," she said.

I was so scared to even talk about it. At first I thought she was joking. But after a while, it started to feel too real, like this was something we were actually planning. When we hung up, I just stood there, replaying the conversation over and over again in my head. Had I just agreed to murder my husband?

Sara decided that it would be best if we kept away from each other. We could talk on the phone but we shouldn't spend too much time together. She was going to do it and when it was done she would tell me. I waited and I waited and I waited. And in that time all kinds of things were running through me head. He was the father of my child. Could I do that to Alexis? Just take her father away from her

because he couldn't keep his dick soft?

I kept calling Sara but she never answered. I don't know where

she was. She had disappeared for weeks. Then she calls me one day out

of the blue. She says, "It's all done. We don't have to worry about it

anymore."

That was it. Really cryptic and quick. And just like that our

friendship went back to usual. I really didn't believe her. There was no

proof. No blood, no nothing. That was around the time when he'd

taken Alexis from school.

See, Alexis is all I have left. *All* I have period. The house is in

Malcolm's name. The cars too. Everything was his. The only thing I

ever got out of that whole fucking relationship was my daughter. She

was my light at the end of the tunnel, the one and only thing I ever felt

like I could truly rely on to always be there. I would give her all the

love nobody else had ever wanted from me. I would protect her with

my life.

And that smug, arrogant bastard just goes in there and takes

her. He walks right into that school reeking of expensive cologne and

designer clothes and takes my baby away from me. He used her like

she was disposable, only there to serve his purpose — which is to make me loathe him with every cell of my being—and then he tossed her

back to me. Here, I'm done with her.

He never paid any attention to her. He never gave her the kind

of love she deserved. And that wasn't fair. What did she do to warrant

that kind of behavior? Was it because of me? Was it because I was her

mother that she had the misfortune to have her daddy walk out on her?

Nowadays, daddy being gone doesn't make you special but it can still

screw you up in special ways.

You wanna know when I knew about Toby and Elizabeth? The

second I held my baby daughter in my arms for the first time. That was

the moment, detectives, when I knew that not only had my husband

been screwing stupid interns, he had fathered my best friend's

children. I mean, how stupid did they think I was? Sara's brother is

only her half brother and the similarities between them are so few and

far between you wouldn't even know they were related. And they

looked like Malcolm. Little Toby had Malcolm's dark eyes, the shape of

his head. Elizabeth had his nose and his eyes. Just like Alexis. The two

of them—*all of them!*—think I'm a goddamn idiot! They think that I

didn't know? I knew before they knew. I knew what Tyra Bettani

wanted the second she showed her face. I knew I would regret it

forever if I let that woman make a bigger fool out of me. I had put up

with that snake in the grass for eight years. Eight years! And she was going to make away with our savings, our house, my future? Oh no.

Couldn't let it happen. Wouldn't let it happen.

Do you know how humiliating it is for everybody to know

your husband is trotting around town on three legs? That he wears his

wedding ring proudly while he sleeps around? He tried to rape me!

Me, his wife. He promised me everything. He promised me wealth, he

promised me anything I could want. And then he tried to take it all

away.

I *hate* him more than you could ever understand. I *hate* him.

And I relive the moment I shot him every single time I close my eyes

because I know in my heart he *deserved* it. He humiliated me again and

again, he flaunted his women in my face. He cheated on me, slept with

my best friend, fathered her kids! That was all the more reason to blow

a hole through his head. He should be glad I took his life because

somebody else would have. He was a bad person.

I gave up my life for this man. It could have been out of love. It

could have been out of obligation. Nonetheless, I had done it and I

expected something in return for my sacrifice. But what did I get?

Where was my reward? Soon enough I found out that there was none. I

did what I had to do. This network of people who claimed to only be

looking out for me, were trying to pull the rug right from under me.

You see why I did this, don't you?

"Yes," said Jacks. "I see why."

"So you tried to frame Sara Mezzano for your crime?" said Roberts.

"No," Kelly said. "I didn't try to frame her. She just somehow got entangled in it. But she's not totally innocent."

"Explain that to us," he said. "Did you put her up to it? Blackmail her?"

"With what?" Kelly laughed. "All I could do was expose her for the liar she was. She knew I was going to kill Malcolm. She just didn't know when. When it was done, I called and told her."

"Which was when?"

"Right after I talked to Agnes. I had to play the grieving widow, right?"

"Right."

"Did Sara kill Tyra Bettani?" Jacks asked.

"Your guess is as good as mine. Sara said she was going to talk to her, to make sure Tyra had no designs on contesting Malcolm's will. Apparently Malcolm had made concessions for Sara, Toby and Elizabeth as well as Tyra and their unborn child."

Roberts leaned in close, his voice a menacing whisper. "Where is Tyra Bettani?"

Kelly met his eyes. For a long moment, they stared at one another. "Why do you think I know where she is?"

Roberts slapped the table with his palm, the sound ricocheting off the walls. "Because you've sat here and you've lied to us from the beginning. You lied about everything. You expect me to believe a cold bitch like you would stop at just one?"

"Detective Roberts, that's enough," Jacks said. He waited until his partner had taken his seat again. "Can you at least tell us where the baby is?"

"I'm not a monster, Detective Jacks," she said. "I'm really not. Sara didn't tell me what happened when she met up with Tyra. She could be dead or she could be living in another state or another country. That's not for me to say."

"Get her outta here," Roberts growled menacingly. "I mean it, or else I'm going to strangle her with my bare hands."

Jacks rounded the table and pulled Kelly up from her seat. "Kelly Stewart, you are under arrest for the murder of Malcolm Stewart. You have the right to remain silent—"

"Oh, that's not a problem, Detective. I've already told you everything."

Faith

Larry Phillips was not a lucky man. He was the sort who waited for things to come to him and if they didn't, he reasoned that he was not meant to have them. Larry didn't have much.

Matilda, his wife, wasn't the sort of woman who made a good wife. She didn't come from good people, which should have been Larry's first hint that their union would never produce any sort of bliss. It seemed the longer they were married, the less they had to say to one another, until there was nothing left to say at all. Now they spent most of their time on either side of the living room. She, watching television. He, gazing into space, thinking, wondering and slowly resigning himself to the hell of his own making.

His son, Jeffrey, personified failure at every turn. He was thirty-one and had never had a job for more than a month. He had fathered at least three offspring but acknowledged none but the boy, for whom he had nothing but a smug smile and a dollar bill. Jeffrey had no respect for Larry and had taken to calling him a bastard beneath his breath, much in the same way his mother did when she thought

Larry was out of earshot. The two of them perched on the couch like crows on a fence line, watching Larry with ill-concealed contempt.

Every day, passengers loaded and unloaded the bus that Larry drove, but he never looked at them. He studied the lines on the ground and the flashing yellow, red and green lights from the traffic signals. He watched the people mill about, as though time would wait for them to catch up, and thought about pressing his foot on the gas and mowing them all down. He tried to drown out the string of expletives he heard from 9 to 5ers who piled in and complained that there was nowhere to sit. The bubbling stew of their musk and heavy perfumes flooded his nostrils and drilled a throbbing pain between his eyes. Sometimes he'd imagine himself slamming hard on the brakes and watching their bodies crash into one another and sail through the windshield like trash thrown from a window. He thought about those things so he wouldn't have to think about what was waiting for him when he got home.

He prayed a lot. A man like Larry had to pray on things to try and make sense of the inequity of it all. He'd fall down on his knees at night and beseech some understanding.

"Lord, you have given me a horrible wife and a horrible son. Please give this old man some kind of happiness before I die."

It was the only thing Larry could do.

One overcast morning, Larry pulled up to one of his regular stops. He sat hunched over the wheel as people filed on, pushed their fare through the slot and showed him their passes. His eyes burned from a sleepless night and he was weary. He was in no mood for the chatter of his passengers and the stop-and-go of traffic. After the last person climbed aboard, he reached over to close the door but paused when he heard a distressed, "Wait!"

She was running toward the bus, her face flushed, her eyes panicked, frantically trying to flag him down. When she hopped on, she panted, "Thank you so much!"

And then he looked up and Larry was instantly taken. It was the symphony The Supremes sang about, the heavenly choir, the parting of the skies, the pounding of his heart. His only regret at that moment in his life was that he couldn't get up and follow her to the back of the bus where she sat and plugged headphones into her ears. All along his route, Larry would look into his rearview mirror and watch her as she stared out the window. She had a very lovely round face with a hint of jawbone on either side. Her cheeks were high and round, but not exaggerated like a cherub's, and her nose was short and fat but not large, like her body.

Her hair was not exceptionally pretty or well-styled and she wasn't dressed well. She wore faded jeans, a black coat covered with white pellets of lint, and a pair of old, decaying sneakers. Those ratty sneakers stuck out like a towering weed in a purple garden. But how most women will walk with an air of confidence and sophistication in heels, she walked that way in those sneakers.

As the days came and went and she flashed her pass and smiled at him, Larry felt himself transforming. He stopped pleading for God to take him in his sleep. He didn't even have a drink or two before bed anymore. He started his mornings with a smile that even Matilda the Hun couldn't rip from his lips. He would playfully slug Jeffrey in the gut or pass him a five spot. They would watch him with utter disgust and sip their coffees and crunch their cereal extra loud so they couldn't hear him humming as he walked out the door.

One rainy day, Larry decided that he would talk to her. She boarded the bus alone at her stop but she didn't move to the back as she usually did. She sat behind him and to the right so that if he turned his head, he could see her. For most of the ride, he fidgeted in his seat and pressed too hard on the brakes. When he turned onto Lexington Avenue near the end of his route and the only other passenger got off, he turned to her and said, "How are you this morning?"

She'd pulled her earphones out and leaned forward a little, her right ear turned to him. "What? I'm sorry, I didn't hear you."

"That's all right," he said, a little sheepish. "I just asked how you were doing today."

"Oh," she said. "I'm okay, I guess."

"Monday blues?" he'd asked, because it had been on a Monday that all this occurred.

"Maybe," she said with a slight shrug. "Just tired, I guess. I wish I could go back home and go to sleep."

"I hear that," he said with a chuckle. "By the time I finish my route, I'm so tired I can hardly keep my eyes open."

They lapsed into silence. He drove with his fingers wrapped tightly around the wheel. She sat quietly, twisting her headphone wire around her finger and staring down at her hands.

"So what do you do?" he'd asked, when they were stopped at a light.

"I work for a daycare center."

"Oh, that's nice. Do you have any kids of your own?"

She'd shaken her head and said, "No."

"You don't sound like you want none either," he said and chuckled again, in spite of himself.

"No, I do," she said, her expression a little pained. "I just don't know if it's meant to be. I'd probably make a lousy mother."

"Now why would you think something like that?"

She shrugged and said, "I'd probably just end up like my parents. I think it's unavoidable."

"Not always," he said.

"I don't know anyone who's a good parent. Or even a good person for that matter. Everyone sucks."

"You seem like a good person."

She'd blushed for a second but then shook her head hard enough to make her dangling silver earrings slap her cheeks. "No. I'm not. I do bad things."

"Now that I don't believe."

"Well, you don't know me, do you?"

They were quiet for the rest of the ride. When Larry pulled up to her stop, he reluctantly pushed the doors open and waited for her to get off. She sat there for a moment, staring down at her hands. Then she looked up at him and smiled a little.

"I didn't mean to be rude. It's just a blah day."

Larry had smiled and nodded. "No problem."

"Okay." She got up and pulled her khaki bag onto her shoulder. "See ya."

"See ya...pretty girl."

For a moment, they stared at each other. Then she grinned and got off the bus.

It seemed foolish that a grown man like him would be mooning after a young thing like her. Foolish, and yet so precisely what was meant to happen, like God Himself sent this girl to him. And Larry believed in God to the infinite power, and His creation of the heavens and earth and man and woman.

In the days that followed, they would sit and talk after the other passengers had gotten off. Larry heard himself telling stories he hadn't thought about in years; his days on the farm in North Carolina, the incident with the horse when he'd been kicked clear across the field, his mama's sickness and the nights and weekends he'd worked to give her a decent funeral, his time in Vietnam after her death, getting shot in the leg, and having to return home with nowhere to go and his daddy nowhere to be found. It felt good telling those stories again, like he'd found the lost chapters of his favorite book. And she'd listened with so much interest. She laughed at some things, frowned at others and expressed sadness over the horrors he'd had to face during the war.

Larry would say that at times it didn't feel like he was talking to a girl young enough to be his daughter. He felt like he was talking to a woman who'd seen and done a lot of things. She, Natalie, seemed so worldly for her age—twenty-four—and spoke so intelligently on just about anything you could bring up. Oftentimes, it made him wish he'd been born thirty years later, just so feeling this way about her wouldn't be wrong.

One morning, as they were coming near her stop and he was finishing up another of his stories, Natalie grinned at him and said, "You're such a fantastic person, Larry. I really like you."

"I really like you too," he'd said.

"I enjoy talking with you so much. You tell the best stories and you're so funny. Your wife is a lucky woman."

"Thank you."

"Maybe if I get lucky, I can meet a guy like you."

He laughed and said, "You still have time, you know."

"Yeah, but the pickings are mighty slim," she said ruefully. "Maybe you're a once-in-a-lifetime type of guy."

When he pulled up to the curb, his hand came up to rest on the door handle. He looked at it, willing it to move before things got out of hand, before that something that he'd felt building in him for weeks came to fruition.

"What's wrong?" she'd said.

At that moment, Larry thought his hearing had gone, because he could hear no sound. There was no traffic, no people. There was only breath and the erratic pounding of his heart.

She rose slowly, her bag dangling from her forearm, her glossy pink lips parted. It seemed to take forever for her to come those two feet and when she did, when she was standing right there before him, he breathed in and caught her scent — lavender and baby powder — and he became lightheaded. His eyelids floated down and he felt their breaths mingling, warming his nose, right before she placed her plump lips against his.

Blood pumped furiously through his body and brought every nerve ending screaming back to life. He cupped her head in his large hands and pulled her closer, pushing his tongue into her mouth as though he were starved for a taste of her. And he was. Night after night, she twisted and writhed her way through the dirtiest dreams he'd ever had. He wanted to touch her like he did in his mind. He wanted to bury himself inside her and die from the wet heat. He wanted her so badly he trembled.

His body buzzed with desire the whole week after. His mind strayed to fantasies of intense lovemaking where she cried out to him as he drove into her. He imagined her shakes and shivers and orgasmic convulsions and his own painful release. Seeing her each morning sent his senses into overdrive and it was all he could do to not pull the bus over at the first motel and take her inside.

When the day came that Larry finally got to make love to her, they met in a movie theater during the matinee, when the theater was nearly empty. She sat far in the back, away from the few people who were there. When he sat down beside her, she didn't wait. She slid her warm hand up his thigh. He clenched it, squeezing her chubby fingers between his before pressing them to his lap. His breath whistled between his teeth. Their eyes met. She wet her lips and slid down his zipper.

They left the theater before the show was over. Her apartment was not far away. On the landing, he leaned against her as she fumbled with the key in the lock. He pressed his lips to her neck and reached around her thick body to knead her breasts. When they got inside, she led him straight to the bedroom. He felt as nervous as a virgin standing before her, his fingers skating over her hard nipples, his heart pounding its way out of his chest. She quickly unzipped his pants and let them fall into a pool around his ankles.

They lay across the bed, Larry on his back, she leaning over him, kissing his quivering body. He heard his own moans as though from far away and closed his eyes. Then she climbed on top of his body and took him inside her. It wasn't long before that terrific pressure built in him and she rocked him closer and closer to the edge until a pounding orgasm was wrenched from his body.

The Lord our God had answered his prayers.

He would meet with her late in the evenings. She would come to the door, a beguiling smile tugging at the corners of her luscious mouth, dressed in a lacy nightgown or just a shirt. The room would be spiced with whatever incense she bought off the street that week. Usually, it was sandalwood. It smelled manly, she would say. Each night, she undressed him, massaged him, kissed him, and then she would lay him down and make love to him the likes of which he hadn't experienced in as many years as she had been alive. And he was happy to surrender to the feelings, happy to drown in his sexual reawakening.

Right now she was snuggled up against his side in a ball like a little kitten. In the dim light, he could see her lips curl into a smile. She sighed dreamily and slid her arm across Larry's wild mat of chest hair, resting her hand over his man breast. Matilda would have given him a pinch or a jiggle and ask if he needed a new bra. But Natalie liked his bosom. She licked them and twisted them with desire. They had just made love and now he was drowsy and sated like a man who'd just eaten a big meal. He leaned back against the pillows to reminisce.

It had been a long time since Larry had been loved well. The last time he'd rolled off Matilda's lumpy mass of a body — November 13, 1999 — he'd lain there, forlorn, staring at the water marks on his ceiling for hours and wondering if he should pay someone to come fix it or if he could do it himself. Matilda was out of bed immediately, washing him away from her genitals and shrouding herself in a muu muu. There was no post-orgasm kiss. There was no snuggling and no words of love. A year later, the ceiling was fixed and an orgasm had become a thing of the past.

After two years had gone, Larry began to ask himself if this was the way it was really meant to be for a man his age. There were always the myths and half-truths, the stories of our sexless fifties and sixties. His daddy had pulled him aside on his wedding day and said, "Lissen here, boy. Havin' a wife ain't the best thing you cudda done. Just don't get too used to a full well."

"Aw, no, Daddy," Larry'd said, his boyish grin bigger than his face. "Tily's a hot one. She'll do anything to please me."

"Ha!" Daddy had laughed. "She a wife now. Them days is ovah."

As the time passed, Matilda's womanly curves acquiesced to dimpled, sagging flesh and the lips that used to be like fluffy pink pillows had flattened and turned down at the corners. Wrinkles etched over her wheat-colored face like roads on a map and her hair was a nappy web of gray and white. Every now and again, Larry would watch her stare into the mirror in their bedroom, seeming to search her face for something familiar. She would pull back the loose skin around her eyes, lift the corners of her mouth and sigh with disappointment when they fell back into loose puddles. Her brow had settled into a natural frown that dipped down the slope of her thin nose. Her back was curved into a firm hunch and she tended to shuffle everywhere now.

This was so for Larry too. Even with his injured knee, his gait had still been sure and quick. Now his knee was acting up all the time and his ankles throbbed with a dull pain. His belly had rounded out to a perfectly shaped ball that blocked the view of his feet. He hadn't lost his hair but the muscles he'd once flexed with pride had softened. The able young man he used to be was giving way to the withered old man he was destined to become. It made him sad and he wore that sadness very heavily upon his face. He felt helpless, and the one and only place where he could still feel like a man was denied him.

By the time Larry had reached his fiftieth year, his spirits were broken well enough that women had become invisible to him. He hadn't even realized that he'd stopped noticing the scent of a woman, the softness, the fullness of body and the promise of head-tingling delights. When had he stopped dreaming of those things and started contemplating death?

Natalie rolled onto her back. Her large, jiggly breasts separated and fell to either side of her body. Larry bent and kissed the nipple of the breast closest to him.

"Do you think I'm pretty?"

"Of course I do," he smiled.

"Do you think I'm beautiful?"

"More than any woman in the world."

"Do you love me?"

He thought about it for a moment. "I don't know if I believe in love," he answered sadly. "It just ain't never worked out for me. How can I think it's true?"

"'Cause it is," she said. "I think it is."

Larry shook his head and said, "I ain't never met nobody who really loved whoever they were with. Nobody. Not my mama, not my daddy. Not any of his wives. My own wife don't even love me and I'm sure, after all this time, I probably don't love her either."

"So why do you stay married to her?"

Larry shrugged. "I don't know. I guess I never got around to leaving for good."

She turned her head to study his face. "Can I call you daddy?" she asked.

He frowned at her. "Why you want to call me daddy?"

"Because," she said, "you'd stay with me. No matter what I did, I know you wouldn't leave."

"What about your real daddy?" he said with a smile. "Wouldn't he mind if you was calling somebody else Daddy?"

"He doesn't care about me," she said with a wave of her hand. "At times I forget he is my daddy. He doesn't love me."

Larry gazed up at the ceiling. His daddy had told him that marriage isn't supposed to be permanent. It's just something you do till the next one comes.

"You don't never fall in love wid no women. Then they think they gotchu. Don't never let 'em getchu, boy. All they do is kick you t'ward the grave."

He supposed he could get over not loving Matilda. But his son, his boy Jeffrey, well, that he couldn't quite reconcile. The boy was almost the spitting image of him. He was tall and broad, like Larry had been in his youth, and just as chocolate brown with the same deep-set eyes and thick, bushy eyebrows. He was a smart boy with many talents he never exercised. He'd quit doing anything he ever started. Including being a father. Larry had little grandchildren out in the world that he'd never get to spoil and bounce on his knee. He'd never get to see if any of them had inherited some of his features or if they were smart or athletic or pretty.

He supposed it was his fault. He should have done a better job at raising the boy. But he had been swamped in misery for too long to care much for anyone else's happiness, least of all his son.

He'd never shown much of an interest in Jeffrey's life, even when he was getting into trouble at school and hanging out with hoodlums. He never told him about women and the responsibilities that went with lying down with them. He never talked to him about hard work or ambition or goals and dreams. He'd never raised the bar off the ground for his only son. How could he have expected the boy to achieve any amount of success when he had done nothing to show him that he could? Maybe he deserved the contempt his son heaped on him because he'd never tried to do any good by him.

Natalie slid her hand down his arm, over his protruding belly, his stocky thighs and around to his back. She pulled him as close as their big bodies would allow and pressed her nose to his neck.

"Your body is so sexy."

"I'm old and flabby," he said. "I can't even stand up for longer than ten minutes without my knee hurting."

"So?" she said, pecking a kiss on his chest. "Sexiness is more than just a muscular body."

"Oh yeah?" he said, looking down into her face. "What else is it?"

She tapped her finger against her chin as she thought. "It's like…the way you carry yourself. Very dignified. And how you look at stuff. Like you can see things other people can't."

"I do that?"

"Yes," she said. "All the time."

All Larry ever saw were all the things he'd done wrong. Things had turned sour so quickly between him and Matilda. It wasn't long after jumping over the broom that she refused to pick up one.

"My mama," she'd said once, "didn't cater to no man and I ain't 'bout to neither. If you want yo suppah and I'm too tired to cook it, you damn well better get it yoself and you better clean every dish you use!"

He'd argued with her, demanded that she do as a wife should do—please her man. She'd laughed at that and informed him that she was going out with her girlfriends and she wouldn't be back anytime soon.

Maybe he'd loved her feistiness and the sparks that used to radiate off her. Maybe he'd only loved lying with her. Or maybe at one time, her no-nonsense attitude and biting words had been the challenge he'd needed. But it'd become tiresome. She was ready to square off with him whenever he opened the door and it made his body ache.

If Matilda knew about Natalie, she'd likely try to kill him. Then she'd divorce him and claim that he'd always been a lousy husband, barely able to make a living, nonexistent in the bedroom, and now, unfaithful as well. She'd take his house and his pension and leave him with only his underwear and the aftertaste of bitter regret.

How unfair, he thought. She had given him the worst thirty-five years of his life and he would be made to suffer for seeking some happiness. What was wrong with the world when a man couldn't leave a woman he didn't want without worrying whether or not he'd end up broke and homeless? She could be angry and hostile and she could accuse him without accusing him of doing all kinds of things and Larry had to take it. He had to because if he got angry, if he defended himself and his right to feel like the man he'd always wanted to feel like, she would take it all away. He was very afraid of that.

Which was why Larry was thinking of calling the whole thing off.

If he just pulled out now, while no one was looking, who would be the wiser? Would Natalie tell? Would she play the woman scorned and rat him out to Matilda? He doubted it. She seemed too sweet in nature to be so malicious. But she was a young girl. And his experience told him that girls her age didn't handle rejection well.

What if she turned to stalking him or calling his home? Or worse, what if someone saw the two of them together?

It had stayed on Larry's mind since the first time they made love. His doubts ebbed and flowed during the weeks since. What did a young girl of her age and experience want with a man like him? What did she see in him?

It could be that she saw everything Larry'd ever wanted a woman to see. Maybe she saw someone who tried to be the best man he could be even though he hated his life. Maybe she saw the big strapping man of his youth, the hard worker, the honest, decent guy. Maybe she knew somehow, in spite of his disinterested parenting and philandering ways, that Larry Phillips really was a good man.

"What are you thinking about?" she asked.

"Nothing," he said. "Just thinking."

"I hate when you tell me you're not thinking about anything."

"Why?"

"Because you are thinking about something. You just don't want to tell me."

Larry sighed and surreptitiously scratched his pubis. "It's not that. It's just...I need to work some things out in my head."

She pulled the covers over her breasts and stared up at the ceiling. "How come your wife is angry with you?"

"I don't know. I don't really want to talk about her."

"Does she know about me?"

"No."

"Why not?"

He turned to her. "Why would she?"

Natalie shrugged and sat up against the pillows. "I don't know. I thought maybe you might have told her."

"Why would I tell her about you?"

"Do you mind if I smoke a cigarette?" She reached over to the nightstand and picked up her pack.

"No." He watched as curls of smoke lifted toward the ceiling. "You didn't answer me."

She folded her fleshy slabs of legs and rocked them from side to side. She chewed her fingernail and took puffs of her smoke. "How can you cheat on your wife?"

Her eyes demanded an answer he didn't have. "Are you mad at me?" he asked.

"I don't know," she said, shrugging like a petulant child. "I just don't get you."

"What don't you get?"

"You!" she shouted, flinging her arms at him. "You seem like such a good person. But you're not. You're just like all the rest of them."

"How?"

"Because you cheat," she said. "You cheat and you don't care."

Larry sat up and fixed the covers over his waist. "I do care."

"Yeah, about you. You care about getting your rocks off with young girls." She snorted and took an angry drag from her cigarette.

"That's not the way it is."

"Whatever," she mumbled.

His eyes burned from guilt as he stared down at his underwear on her floor. "You're too young to understand, that's all."

"Oh, whatever," she snapped. "I'm not stupid."

"Maybe you are," Larry said, his voice rising a bit. "You knew I was married." He shoved his hand in front of her face. "That's a wedding band, sweetheart."

She slapped his hand away. "I know what it is."

For a long while the only sounds in the room were her sharp puffs on her cigarette. Then he felt her cool hand on his arm.

"It's just confusing."

"What is?"

"Men. Relationships. Life. I don't get it. I don't think I ever will." She paused for a moment. "It's like my father. I don't get him at all."

"It's hard to be a man," Larry said, staring down at his rough, chapped hands. "It's a lot harder than anybody thinks."

"What's so hard about being there for someone you love?"

Larry said nothing.

"Don't you have a son?" she asked.

"Yes."

"What's his name?"

"Jeffrey."

"What's he like?"

Larry tilted his head back to rest on his shoulders. He sighed deeply and pulled the word from his chest: "Disappointing."

"Why?"

Larry blinked to clear his blurry eyes. "I don't know. Probably a lot of good reasons."

"But you still love him though. Right? I mean, in spite of it all, you still love your son?"

Larry wanted to feel that warmth in his chest whenever he looked at his son. He wanted to take pride in Jeffrey's accomplishments, what little of them there may be. But he always felt like something was missing there that he wasn't sure he could find.

Larry's daddy had divorced his mother when he was Larry's age. Within a month, he was remarried to a girl younger than Larry, whom he left after four months. Then he picked up with a woman closer to his own age and married her after three weeks. He left her too. His daddy was the sort of man who didn't like to put down roots. He'd chased skirts right up until the day he died — January 15, 1989 — and left Larry with nothing but a legacy of bad debts and a string of angry ex-wives fighting like alley cats over the pieces of his carcass. Larry hadn't seen him once in the four years before his passing. He'd given up on him. If you didn't have breasts, daddy had no time for you.

"I have to, don't I?"

She lit another cigarette. "I don't know. Do you?"

Larry shrugged. He reached down and picked up his underwear and pulled them on.

"Are you leaving?"

"No. Just going to the bathroom."

Larry pulled open her bedroom door and limped to the bathroom. He'd been lying down too long and his ankles were aching. His chest ached some too and he rubbed it while he used the toilet. When he returned to bed, she was still smoking and staring at nothing.

"I'm sorry," she said. "I didn't mean to get all in your face."

He climbed under the covers and reclined. "It's all right. Don't worry about it."

"I really hate my father."

She was crying. Tears collected under her chin and dripped onto the sheet. She took a drag from her cigarette and flicked the ash on the floor.

"He's such a bastard," she went on. "He doesn't care about me and I don't know why." She laughed a little. "I guess I shouldn't feel too hurt because he doesn't care about his other kids either. He just moves wherever he needs to at whatever time he needs to do it. And he doesn't think about what he's left behind. Whenever he does come by to see me, he only stays long enough to ask for money and then he's gone again. I haven't seen him in so long. Days, weeks, months, years maybe."

There had been so many times when Larry had considered leaving Matilda, so many times when his bag was packed and his hand was on the doorknob. Only twice did he actually make it out the door. But both times he came back.

Jeffrey had been no more than three the first time Larry had walked out on Matilda. His memory still bore the image of Jeffrey standing in the kitchen in his cowboy pajamas, one of his toys stuck under his arm, his face glistening with tears as he sobbed hysterically for Larry not to go. Matilda was screaming at the boy to go back to his room as she tried to pull the suitcase from Larry's hand. But he'd held on, like he'd held onto his resolve to not take crap from her anymore. He'd been firm and for the first time he'd meant it.

"I'm a man!" he'd shouted. "I deserve respect! I put food on the table! I keep this roof over our heads! When you gon' give me my respect?"

"When you earn it," she'd shouted right back in his face. "When you do somethin' to prove you a husband to me and a daddy to that boy besides sitting yo fat ass on the couch! Until then, you ain't got nothin' to say to me!"

"Then I'm leaving," he said, yanking the suitcase away from her.

"Oh no you ain't," she said, getting between him and the door. "You not gon' leave me to fend for myself when you the one who put me here in the first place! I swear I'll kill you first."

"Try it," he'd growled. "Just try it."

He'd looked over his shoulder at Jeffrey. He was sitting on the floor, his stomach convulsing with sobs, his mouth yawning as he screamed, "No, Daddy! Noooo!"

Then Larry turned and walked out the door.

"Sometimes I wish he would die."

"Who?"

"My father." Natalie looked at him as she wiped tears from her cheeks. "Were you listening?"

He rubbed his chest again. "Yeah. Sorry. I was just thinking about something."

"Oh." She dragged off her cigarette again. "That's wrong, isn't it? To wish somebody dead? You shouldn't wish anybody dead. It's bad karma."

"We all say things we don't mean sometimes."

"Do you?"

"Of course."

"Like when you told me you liked me?"

He frowned and said, "I didn't lie about that. I do like you."

"But you don't love me."

He sighed. "I told you how I feel about that."

"It sounds like a lie," she said. "It sounds like something somebody says when a person says I love you and they don't want to say it back. Like when a guy says, 'It's not you. It's me.' But it's always you."

"I care about you," he offered.

She looked away and said nothing.

"I don't get it. What do you want me to say?"

"Do you just sleep with people that you feel nothing for?" she snapped.

"Not since my youth," he said with a smile.

"I don't think that's a cool thing to do," she said, folding her meaty arms over her breasts. "You shouldn't have sex with people you don't care about."

"You never slept with somebody just to satisfy a need?"

She looked him straight in the eyes. "No."

"Well, you're still young. You've got time."

"Would you stop telling me that! You don't know that. You don't know how much time I have or you have or anyone has." She paused. "You don't want to be with me?"

"I am with you."

She became exasperated. "You know what I mean, Larry."

His shoulders bunched with tension. He sat up and tried to relax them. "I think it's time for me to go."

"Please don't go," she said as he stepped into his pants. "Just ignore me."

"It's about time I left anyway," he said.

"No, please," she pleaded, throwing aside the blanket and leaping for him. "Just stay another half hour. Please. I hate it when you leave."

He removed her hands gently and kissed her cheek. "I'll be back, sweetheart. Promise."

"I don't want your promises. People don't keep promises," she said and threw her body back onto the sheets. She yanked the covers up over her head.

"Natalie," he chided. "Come on, now. Stop acting like a kid."

"Leave me alone."

Larry slipped on his shoes and buttoned up his shirt. "I'll come back. Okay?"

When she finally emerged from the blankets, her eyes were shiny with tears. "I'm such a mess. Every time I think I've got it together, I lose it again."

"It's okay," Larry said. He touched his forehead and sweat came off onto his fingers. "You'll be all right, Natalie. You're a smart woman."

She turned away. "Thank you."

Larry sat down on the edge of the bed. He reached for her hand but she pulled it away.

"Will you come back tomorrow?" she asked.

"Yes."

"Really?"

"Yes."

She nodded but still refused to meet his eyes. He cupped her chin in his palm and turned her face back to him. "I'm sorry."

"For what?" she asked.

"'Cause I can't give you what you want."

She pulled his hand from her face. "I don't think anybody can."

Larry heaved a great sigh and pushed himself up off the bed. He pulled on his coat.

"All I ever wanted," she said, "was for somebody to love me. I'm tired of waking up by myself and going to bed every night alone. Nobody comes, nobody calls. It's just me. And I *hate* that so much."

She climbed out of bed and pulled on a shirt and jeans. "I'll walk you to the door."

At the door, Larry leaned down and placed a soft kiss on her forehead. "You won't be lonely forever. I promise you that."

"I don't believe in promises." She closed the door and turned the locks.

Larry left her building and started down the street. It was a cold, crisp evening. The purple sky was dotted with white stars and the moon sat behind a mist of gray clouds. The dead autumn leaves caught

on the breeze and ushered him down the street. He walked with his

hands tucked into his pockets, his head bowed to the wind. Now that

Larry was outside, he was sweating more than he had when he was

inside. He stopped for a moment and looked back at her building. He

could see the light from her bedroom from there. She moved past it as

she pulled her shirt over her head. Then the lights went out.

The thought of returning home to Matilda made him feel tired.

She was probably sitting on the couch right now watching the evening

news and chatting on the phone to one of her girlfriends. Jeffrey was

probably sitting right beside her, staring at nothing, thinking about

nothing, being nothing. The house would be dim but the glow from the

kitchen light would spotlight the couch, leaving the rest of the house

shrouded in shadows. He was glad for that. He wouldn't want them to

see his face when he came in.

Larry stopped at a liquor store and bought a pack of cigarettes.

He lit one before he left the store, hoping it would calm his nerves a

little. He wiped more sweat from his brow and massaged his churning

stomach. He stood on the street and smoked, watching the store front

lights of China Wok blink from across the street. A pudgy little Chinese

woman moved around inside, neatly arranging table settings and

shouting over her shoulder to the man behind the counter. He came around it, pulled her close and bent her over his arm for a dramatic kiss. She swatted at him and returned to her table settings, grinning at him over her shoulder.

He took a puff. The kind of life he'd always dreamt of was just an overactive imagination at work. Love like he wanted didn't exist. He should leave Matilda and Jeffrey, because they would probably be happier that way anyhow, and he should go somewhere and start a new life. It was too late for him to try and be whatever it was he'd always wanted to be. The fire that had to live and breathe in him in order to do that was gasping for its last breaths.

He took another puff. He rubbed his chest and leaned against the brick wall beside the liquor store. He wiped sweat from his brow.

There was never a time when Larry Phillips wasn't miserable. From the time he was a kid, watching as his father beat and berated his mother and brought different women under her roof, to now as a grown old man, leaving the home of his young mistress to return to a woman he couldn't stand. He'd never wanted to be like his daddy. He'd hated him. Every time he'd pull up in his Buick with one of his ladies, every time he'd slapped some money in Larry's palm as he was walking out the door and every time he promised something and never came through, Larry hated him more. Now, somehow, in spite of all his

efforts, he was him, the man he despised and loved. At times, he
couldn't figure out which emotion he felt more.

This was how Larry's life had worked out. There wasn't a
thing he could do about it now. He would have to go on driving his
bus everyday. He would have to keep going back home to Matilda and
Jeffrey because that's where he belonged. He didn't belong with
Natalie. She was a sweet girl and he enjoyed all the time they'd spent
with one another, but she wanted so much from the world, from him,
and there was no way he could give it to her.

He understood her pain. He understood wanting so much
from everyone around you and receiving so little. He'd loved Matilda
very much. He'd fallen for her right away. But she had never loved
him. When he thought about it now, he figured she had probably
married him just because she wanted to be married. He loved Jeffrey
too. Larry could still remember how he'd smelled the first time he'd
held him and he remembered his dark eyes as he stared up at him. He
hadn't cried or squirmed. He'd looked up at Larry and Larry had
looked down at him and his heart ached from feeling so much love.

He puffed his cigarette and tossed it aside. He bent forward
and took a deep, wheezing breath and pressed hard as he rubbed his
chest. The lights from China Wok were blurring. His knees threatened
to buckle. Larry slid down to the cold ground.

It had been that moment, that brief space in time with his son in his arms that he had struggled to find again. Not just in Jeffrey or Matilda or Natalie even. But in life. He'd always get close enough to touch before it was snatched away. This was how it was and this was how it would always be.

Every Sunday he sat amongst the congregation and praised the Lord and hallelujahed and tithed and did communion. But it hadn't done any good. Nothing had changed. Nothing ever would.

A tear rolled down Larry's cheek. His fingers curled into his chest as a burning pain lashed across it.

Tomorrow, when he awoke, Matilda would be in the kitchen, stirring her instant coffee in a mug, humming a church hymn, glad that he wasn't awake yet. Jeffrey would stumble out of his room and into the bathroom. Outside, the newspaper would slap against the front door. The morning news would come on and fill the house with lively chatter. And Larry would sit on the edge of his bed, his feet halfway in his slippers, his head hanging down, not sure if he was ready to face another day.

He would think of Natalie and wonder what she could say today that would make him smile. He would relive the taste of her on his tongue and the coolness of her sheets on his skin. He'd close his eyes and remember her smile. Then, maybe, he would smile. And maybe he would be inspired to get out of bed with a renewed sense of hope. But memories will always fade and his heart would continue to sink into the pool of his stomach. Larry will wonder how much longer this will go on.

Now, here on a quiet street corner, with the neon lights of storefronts blinking and blurring before him, Larry started to think that maybe it wouldn't be too much longer. His breathing became shallow and when his body fell over, he pressed his cheek to the cool cement.

"Lord...help me..."

A spasm of pain gripped his body in a tight vise. Tears slid across the bridge of his nose and dripped onto the ground. He let his eyes close. And, with the last breath in his body, Larry whispered:

"Father."

Gladys in the Bar

Even though it had been nearly fifteen years since Maggie had divorced him, Rufus still drove up the driveway of her house every afternoon at noon to take her on her errands. Maggie knew when he was outside so he never had to honk. She always took her time coming out, carrying that ugly knitted bag she'd gotten from her new boyfriend and walking with her hand extended daintily, as if he were there holding it up for her. She had started to wear make up, something Rufus noted and pointed out a few months ago. That's when she'd told him oh so nonchalantly that she was now seeing someone who happened to think she looked very pretty with it on. Rufus snorted at that. No woman looked good with her face covered in paint. At least not to him. He told her she should take it off and stop being ridiculous. She refused to speak to him. Still, he showed up every day for her errands.

Today he pulled in earlier than usual. He'd been out taking care of business at the bank and decided to come for her early since her house and the bank were a short distance apart. A car was sitting in his spot in the driveway. He parked along the curb and made his way across the lawn, limping on his sore foot. He used his key to go inside

even though he knew Maggie did not like it when he did that. She was

playing Ella Fitzgerald with the volume low. The house smelled like

her chicken and dumplings. Her shoes were under the coffee table. He

smiled when he saw the photo from their 38th anniversary dinner still

sitting on the mantle. That had been their last anniversary. The

following day, Maggie had told him she wanted a divorce.

He heard a noise upstairs and made the slow climb up. She'd

turned the children's rooms into guest bedrooms. The doors stood

open, the rooms empty except for beds, dressers and nightstands. Each

of their three children lived in different states. They communed on

holidays and at funerals with the occasional phone call here and there.

Rufus would wager that Maggie heard from them more than he did.

He had taken a bulk of the blame during the divorce.

Maggie's bedroom door was closed. He heard the noise again,

like a soft shout, and pushed the door open. There was Maggie lying

on the bed with some wrinkled old bastard humping the daylights out

of her. Her eyes were rolled back into her head, her legs were pointing

toward Heaven and her mouth was slack. They kept on going,

obviously unaware that they were being watched. He kept calling out

"Oh Maggie, baby!" and she could barely get his name out. Rufus

thought he would be sick. He eased out of the room, closed the door and made his way down the stairs and back out to the car. He sat there for a long time, just waiting. Finally, the front door opened and that old wrinkled bastard (now fully clothed) came out, got into the car in the driveway and drove away. She came out a few minutes later, smiling from ear to ear. She got into the car and pulled down the overhead mirror to straighten her hair. When she noticed that Rufus hadn't started the car yet, she looked at him and said, "Why are we still sitting here?"

"Get out of my car."

"What?"

"You heard me. Get out of my car."

"Rufus, what—"

He whipped around to face her. "Why don't you ask George to take you on your goddamn errands? We're not married anymore and I'm sick of this."

Rufus reached across and opened her door, grabbed her purse and tossed it out on the street. She could barely speak as she climbed out to pick up the personal items that had fallen out and scattered in the street. Rufus drove away.

He found himself at the end of a bar, sucking on a whiskey and Coke while sad country music twanged in the background. What a stupid bastard he'd been! For years and years, he sat around like a lumpy old sack waiting for her to forgive him, give him another

chance. Maybe they wouldn't remarry, but at least they wouldn't be so

damn hostile. Now she was screwing old George and wearing make up

and Rufus didn't know what to do.

He could go out and screw too. Everything still worked. Right

after they divorced he did do a lot of screwing. He'd only dated one

lady for a long time until she passed away suddenly. That's when he

got to thinking about Maggie again, the kind of woman she'd been and

what he needed at that time in his life. But to her he was only good for

taking her to doctor's appointments and grocery shopping. Well, those

days were done. He was his own man, had been for fifteen years. Now

it was time for him to own that and stop waiting around for things that

would never come. After all, what did he have to lose by having a

friendly romp with an obliging stranger?

He surveyed the bar. The trouble was that there were too many

young faces. All the girls looked like girls and the old women looked

like old women. He didn't want to screw a lady with a gray bush. If he

was going to do it, he wanted it to at least be enjoyable enough.

He tapped the bar. "Young fella?"

The bartender came over to him. "What can I do for you, old

timer? You want another whiskey and Coke?"

"What I want is a nice screw. You think you could help me out with that?"

"Yeah, sure. Screwdriver coming up."

"No, no." Rufus waved him back. "I know what a screwdriver is and I don't want that. I want a screw. A nice, willing lady without any venereal diseases."

"Seriously?"

"One hundred per cent."

The bartender shrugged and said, "All right. Well, if you go in the back and knock three times on the door, that's where Gladys lives."

"Is she old?"

"To me she is," he said.

"Look, young fella. I've got three kids old enough to be one of your parents. Just answer my damn question."

"She's like fifty. Or something. I don't know."

"Does she do this kind of thing often?"

"She has a few friends. She's a nice lady. Not nasty at all."

"That's all I needed to hear."

Rufus left some money on the bar and carried his whiskey and Coke into the back. A group of guys were playing pool. There was a door with a frayed, old war-time advertisement taped onto it. Rufus knocked three times and the door opened immediately. A gray-haired lady in a purple peignoir opened the door. He could see her breasts between the opening, sagging and pointing in opposite directions. Her face was a wrinkled old sheet in the unflattering light.

"Are you Gladys?"

"Who wants to know?"

"Rufus."

She smiled real slow and nasty. She hollered over her shoulder, "Gladys! You know some old fart named Rufus?"

"Does he have money!" she shouted back from some unseen place.

The woman looked at him as if to say, "Well, do you?" Rufus took fifty dollars from his wallet.

"He's good!" the woman shouted back to Gladys. She stepped aside and tossed her head toward a beaded curtain with soft red lighting beyond it where Gladys lay in wait. The ice in his whiskey and Coke rattled against the glass. He set it down on an empty bookshelf.

When he pulled back the curtains, he saw Gladys lying on a low, unmade bed. She was wearing a blue nightshirt and her hair was up in curlers. A limp smoke was stuck between her brown lips. She put it out in the ashtray and set aside her tabloids that she had been reading.

"How do I know you?" she asked, looking him up and down.

"You don't."

"Damn right, I don't. I don't usually do it with old timers like you."

Rufus started feeling a little self-conscious and straightened his seersucker jacket. "How old are you?"

"Now, that's none of your damn business, is it?" Gladys let out a loud cackle. "So you wanna fuck or what? It's fifty bucks."

Rufus started undressing and when he was naked, he slid beneath her sheet. It smelled like smoke and pungent perfume. Gladys got up and pulled her panties off. She took the curlers out of her black hair and tossed them on the floor. She lit another cigarette and got into bed beside him. He got a glimpse of her derriere before she pulled the sheet over her too. It was still quite firm but dimpled from cellulite.

"No anal, Pops."

"That's okay."

"If you want oral sex then it's fifteen extra dollars."

"Okay."

"You want it or not?"

"Um...yeah."

She sighed with irritation. "I gotta go take my teeth out. Be right back."

Rufus stared at the water stained ceiling. The crystal chandelier hanging over the bed was dusty and draped in cobwebs. There was a draft coming in from the window across the room. He would tell her to close it when she came back.

Gladys was in the bathroom for a long time. When she came back, she had condoms. "I still get my friend every month. Unless you're shooting blanks?"

"I don't think so."

She started stroking him a little too roughly. He asked her to ease up a bit and she snapped at him that she knew what she was doing. He could barely feel it when she started giving him oral. He told her that.

"That's because you're wearing a condom, Pops. I don't know where you've been sticking this thing." She went back to blowing him.

Rufus couldn't stop thinking about Maggie's drunken eyes as old George gave it to her. He kept getting soft and Gladys got angry. Finally, she climbed on top of him and pushed him into her warm hole. She felt pretty good and the more she rocked over him, the more distant his memory of Maggie and old George got. Still, he couldn't come and Gladys was getting tired.

"What the hell is wrong with you?" she snapped. "Come!"

"I'm trying," he said.

Finally, Gladys gave up and lay next to him. She was sweating buckets and none too happy about it. "I sweated out my curls!"

"I'm sorry."

"I thought you wanted to screw," she said.

"I do…I just have a lot on my mind."

Gladys rolled her eyes. "Whatever. We're not married so I don't care."

Rufus thought about Maggie's face when he'd thrown her purse out of the car. He doubted she would ever forgive him for any of it. He was a cad today and, if he were going to be honest, he'd always been a cad. Everything had had to be his way and that made Maggie miserable.

The reality was that Maggie was screwing old George because Rufus had stopped caring about her and she knew it and that's when she started getting angry. They fought all the time and when they weren't fighting, they were quiet and hostile. The week before their 38th anniversary, the tension inexplicably eased. There were no more questions and accusations. No more crying and threats to leave. Rufus thought he was in the clear again. Then the day after their anniversary dinner, she dropped the bomb on him. He hadn't seen it coming.

Gladys was lighting a cigarette. "You don't get do-overs. Unless you're willing to pay more."

"I don't have more."

"Then I'm afraid it's time to go, Pops."

Rufus got up and dressed. He sat down to put his shoes on and stayed there for a long time.

"Hey." Gladys gave him a nudge with her foot. "Wake up, old timer."

"I'm not asleep," he said. He dropped his shoe. "I just realized that I screwed up my life."

"Join the rest of us," she said wryly. "We meet every Wednesday for dollar fifty drinks till 12."

"How did you screw up your life?" he asked, turning to face her.

At first Gladys seemed offended. Then she sighed and said, "I started doing guys to feed my kid. Then my kid died and I kept doing guys."

"I'm sorry," he said. "How old was your child?"

"He was four," she said. She took a puff of her smoke and went to a mini-fridge in the corner by the bathroom door. She took out a beer. "His name was Ian."

"I have three children," Rufus said. "They don't really like me much."

"Why? You screw around on their mother?"

"Among other things."

"Don't beat yourself up about it, old timer. All guys sleep around on their wives. Nobody's monogamous."

"I wanted to be," Rufus said, a rueful smile pulling at his lips.

"Well, you all want to be," she said. "None of you can quite manage it. Most guys get insulted when you accuse them of thinking with their dicks but ask them what they were using while they screwed around: the head or the dick?"

"I only did it once. I didn't even fuck the girl. She went down on me. I started having second thoughts."

"Before or after you shot your load?"

Rufus laughed ruefully. "After."

"Ha." Gladys smiled and took a swig of beer. "Why'd you go with the girl?"

Rufus tried to remember. "I'm not entirely sure. Things run together in my head. I'm too old to have a clear memory."

"I envy you, old man," she said. "I remember too much. When I was a kid this perv with a hard-on for little girls with fat butts grabbed mine. He actually smiled at me afterwards. Like it was our little secret."

"That's horrible."

She shrugged. "Story of my life. They all only want one thing. Even my father believed I was only good for that."

"Your father molested you?"

"No," she said. "But he treated me like all I was good for was letting some asshole pump me up with a bastard."

"I'm sure he didn't mean to."

"What do you know about it?"

They sat for a time, not speaking. Gladys smoked and chugged beer. Rufus stared at a pair of her panties on the floor.

"I still love her."

"That's pretty obvious."

"Is it?"

"Why else would you be fucking some old broad in the back of a bar? I told you that you men are simple creatures. She's probably got a boyfriend and it's pissing you off."

"I didn't expect it to."

"I'm sure you didn't."

"Can you stop being glib for a minute?" he snapped.

"No."

Rufus sighed. "I don't know what to do. We've been divorced for fifteen years. I don't even know how to talk to her anymore."

"You still loved her when you got rid of her?"

"She divorced me, not the other way around."

"Ha! Now it makes even more sense."

"We had some tough times," he said. "I wish we'd have worked on them a little more instead of just…"

Gladys came to sit beside him. "Can I ask something?"

Rufus nodded.

"Why now do you want her back?"

"I saw her screwing the other guy."

Gladys nodded. "So I was right."

"Yes."

She took one last puff of her smoke and dropped it into her beer can. "I gotta wash my cooch before the next guy gets here. I'll take my sixty-five bucks now."

Rufus gave her the money.

"Good luck getting your wife back," she said.

"Thanks, sweetheart."

She smiled at him a little and went into the bathroom.

Rufus left the bar and headed back to Maggie's. When he pulled up at the house, Maggie and old George were standing on the porch talking. Her hand was lying against his chest and she was leaning close, smiling widely. Old George was looking at her in a way that made Rufus's stomach sink. He kissed her then and Rufus drove

away.

Hi

Whoa. I can't feel my fingers anymore.

I should sit down for a second. No, wait. Maybe if I keep standing my fingers will come back. Then, if my fingers come back, they might be able to convince my feet to come back too. All right. Let's give this a try.

Okay, not bad. I don't feel my fingers coming back yet but my toes are starting to wake up. It feels kinda good.

Mmmmmm....

All right. Just keep going. Walk. Walk. Walk, walk, walk. Left, right, left. Wiggle those toes. Okay, this is good. Now, Feet, tell Fingers to get back here. I'm serious. Tell my fingers to get back here right now.

Why?

What do you mean why? If Fingers don't come back, how the hell am I going to open the door to go outside?

Yeah, didn't think about that one did you, Smart Guy?

Sorry, I didn't mean to be condescending.

Okay...I'm pulling on this door but it will not opeeeeeen. Keep trying. Harder. Harder! Careful though. Don't pop the knob off. Okay, I see the problem. I should be pushing instead of pulling.

Aaaaaaaaaahhhh!!! Fresh air smells good.

Mmmm…it smells like pretzels out here. And dog shit. Fuck! Feet, you were supposed to be on the lookout. One more slip up and I'm cutting you off.

Okay, I'm walking. That air feels good. It's warm and cold at the same time, like opening a freezer on a hot day. Is somebody calling me? Oh, he meant that person. Is that person staring at me? Look away. Don't make eye contact. Just keep moving. Steady sidewalk…steady…

Aww man. Why did I do that? I should have said hello. I'm going to go back and say hello.

"Hi."

"Wassup?"

Okay, now go.

What time is it? Fish don't have a concept of time. They just swim in their bowls. I'm swimming in my bowl. Where are all the other fish? Oh, there's one. That one's wearing a yellow slicker. Funny, I never thought fishes would need rain slickers. I'm going to say hi to that fish.

"Hi."

Oh, maybe he didn't see me. "Hi again."

Why'd he just swim off like that? Oh well. Here's another fish coming up. This one is a girl fish and she's got big red lips. She's a sexy fish.

"Hi, sexy fish."

"Excuse me?"

That's how it is with most sexy fish. They get mad at you for calling them sexy.

Some fish move too fast. How can I say hi to them if they move too fast?

Feet, what do you say we just stand here and wait for the fishes to pass by and then say hi? Sound good? Great.

"Hi."

"Hello."

"Hi."

"Hey."

"Hi."

"How you doing?"

"Hi."

"Whatever."

"Hi."

"Good evening."

We'll stay out here as long as we need to, Feet. We're going to say hi to every person in the world.

But every person in the world doesn't live here. So I guess that means we'll have to go all around the world.

You're tired? Well, I'm tired too. It's hard work trying to stay on top of you.

Rest? How selfish of you! There are millions of people out there waiting to be greeted!

It's starting to get quiet out here. I haven't seen a car in a while. Maybe we should find someplace where people are. What do you mean dangerous? I'm fine. Look, I don't even think people are fish anymore. Hey, let's go into that bar over there.

Whoa. It's dark in here. "Hi."

What's her problem?

"Hi."

Hmm. I don't think that was called for. Here, let's sit at the bar so you can get off my back for a few minutes.

"Hello."

"You want something?"

"No. Just hello."

"Whatever. Don't start any shit."

Jeez. What is wrong with everyone in here? This lady looks nice. "Hi."

"Hi."

"You're friendly. That's nice."

"You're friendly too."

"I know. I'm saying hi to everybody I see."

"Cool...Why?"

"Why not?"

I want a beer. Do I have money? Fuck. I left my wallet somewhere.

"Would you happen to have—"

"Hey buddy."

"Hi."

"Do you have a reason to be talking to my lady?"

"I was just asking for—"

"What? Some ass? How about I kick *your* ass?"

"What?"

"You heard me, bitch. Keep looking at me and I'm going to kick your teeth down your throat."

"But—"

"I warned you."

Ow. Shit. That hurt. I've never been punched in the face before. Especially for nothing. All right, let's get up and get the fuck outta here.

"You want some more?"

"I —"

Fuck! Why'd he hit me again? I didn't even say anything. I know, Feet, I know. But you're going to have to do most of the work.

Yeah, you're right. We never should have left the house.

Rumble in Whispering Gardens

I'm not one of those white guys who are afraid of black guys.
And I'm not one of those wannabe assholes walking around with their
pants around their calves singing rap records and pouring forty ounces
of malt liquor on the curb. I'm a simple guy who likes the simple life I
live. I've got a nice house in a decent neighborhood, a great job as an
equity analyst, a beautiful wife and three kids; two of them too young
to give a crap about Piff Daddy or Puff Diddy or whatever the hell his
name is this week.

As co-chairman of the Neighborhood Unity Group, it's my job
to help welcome new families to our block. Normally we'll set up the
pit, get some Springsteen blasting through the speakers and have
ourselves a good time. It was just Whispering Gardens' way of saying,
"Howdy! And welcome to the neighborhood!"

On the day the Johnsons moved in, I crossed the street of our
cul-de-sac and knocked on the door. I should have known something
was up when I heard the rap music. But I was willing to reserve

judgment because my wife, Carolyn, has relatives from Jersey who do that sort of thing.

A black guy in jeans and a Polo shirt opened the door. He was clean shaven with fat rounding out his jaw. The only thing that kept him from looking like a teenager was the gray hairs on his scalp. "Excuse me," I said. "I'm looking for the owners of this house."

"You're looking at one of them," the guy said and grinned.

"You're the Johnsons?"

"That's right," he said. "How can I help you?"

I cleared my throat and offered my hand and said, "I'm Dave. I live right across the way there. Just wanted to come welcome you to the neighborhood."

He shook my hand and said, "Nice to meet you, Dave. I'm Tyrone but you can call me Ty."

"All right," I said. "Good to meet you, Ty. How do you like Whispering Gardens so far?"

He shrugged and reached up to scratch his chin. "It's all right. Bet you can't get any good soul food around here, but it's cool."

"Well, no…but I think…well, I don't know…"

Tyrone laughed and lightly punched my arm. "I'm just fucking with you, Dave. I'm sure Whispering Gardens isn't a hot spot for collard greens."

"Oh," I said. "Well, uh, listen. I'm the president of N.U.G. —

the Neighborhood Unity Group — and we usually have a party for new

families who move into the neighborhood. We'd like to throw one for

you and yours."

"Oh yeah," he said. "That's cool."

"Okay then. Me and the guys'll get together and plan and I'll

give you a call."

"Cool. Catch you around, Dave." He closed the door.

I crossed over to our house and joined Carolyn on the lawn.

She was kneeling on the ground digging into her flowerbed.

"Hey," she said, glancing up at me before turning back to her

geraniums.

"Our new neighbors are black."

"I could see that," she said dully. "Are they nice?"

I shrugged and very seriously I said, "I know one thing. I

better not start seeing a whole bunch of gangsters hanging out there.

We're gonna keep this neighborhood safe."

Carolyn sighed and shook her head. "He hasn't even done

anything and you're already getting your feathers ruffled."

"I know what's coming, Carolyn," I said.   "I grew up

around blacks. I know how they are."

"Excuse me, Malcolm X."

I waved my hand at her and went inside. Theo, my oldest boy, was in the kitchen making a sandwich. He was a handsome sixteen year-old kid and taller than me by nearly a foot. Lately he'd been walking around with his headphones glued to his head, occasionally saying things like "Go shorty! It's your birthday!" Whatever that meant. I don't understand half the crap these kids listen to nowadays.

"Hey, son," I said, lifting the headphones off his ears.

"Wassup, dad," he said. "How was work?"

"It's work, that's for sure," I said, grabbing a beer. "Is school okay? You getting good grades?"

He nodded. "For shizzel."

I turned to him and frowned. "Excuse me?"

He laughed and said, "Nah, dad. It's just a saying. It means for sure."

I shook my head, mildly annoyed. "I don't like you listening to all that hip hop and rap. You should go through my record collection. I bet you'll find something you like in there."

He gave me a weird look before taking his sandwich into the living room.

After dinner, Carolyn cleaned up while I called the members of N.U.G. over for our weekly meeting. Steve was the first to arrive and joined Carolyn and me in the kitchen. When he moved to the neighborhood about five years ago, he and I hit it off right away. Our families had dinner together frequently. He liked my kids and his wife and Carolyn got along pretty well. But when she left him about a year ago, he took it really hard. Carolyn would bring him dinner and make sure he was taking care of himself and the house. I invited him out for drinks or on fishing trips that me and a few other guys went on every month. He seemed to be doing a lot better these days. If you asked me, he was better off. He'd regained ownership of his dignity and his balls in one fell swoop.

"So you must have met the new family," Steve said as he shoveled the petrified turkey from last night's dinner into his mouth.

"Oh, I met him all right."

"What's that mean?" He glanced uncertainly at Carolyn.

Carolyn muttered something beneath her breath and said, "It means that they're black and Dave's being an ass."

"Black, huh?" Steve said, giving up on the unpalatable food. "Been a long time since we had a black family on the block."

"I know. I'm anticipating problems."

Steve swigged his beer and belched, making his newly rounded belly shake like a Jell-O mold. "Why? Did he say something?"

I waved my hand. "Ah, nothing big. He made some wisecrack about not being able to find soul food in this neighborhood."

The doorbell rang and Carl and Bruce came into the kitchen. Bruce lumbered in like the Jolly Green Giant, his enormous gut swelling over his pants. He lived down the block in a two-story brick house with his wife, Judy, the nosiest woman I've ever met. They moved to Whispering Gardens about twelve and a half years ago, after their youngest had gone off to college. We formed N.U.G. about seven years ago.

Carl was a short, squirrelly looking guy. He had lost most of his hair before leaving his twenties and now had a shiny bald scalp. He was as thin as a pike, his clothes draping over him like they would from a hanger. He lived three houses over, at the center of the cul-de-sac with his wife Linda. One of their four daughters was still living at home. Carl joined N.U.G. to get out of the house and away from Linda's nagging. It wasn't unusual to hear them shouting at one another in the driveway in the mornings or on the front lawn in the evenings. He was younger than Bruce and I by about seven years but looked older by at least fifteen.

I offered them beers and we took our meeting out to the patio.

I took my position in the center of the semi-circle and clapped my hands for silence. "All right, guys. Our only order of business tonight is the welcoming party for the Johnsons, our new neighbors."

"Did you meet them yet?" Carl asked.

"Oh yeah," I said and snorted again. "I met them all right."

"What's that mean?" Bruce asked, laughing a little.

"They're black," Steve said.

Carl and Bruce exchanged a look before bursting into laughter. Bruce slapped a twenty into Carl's open palm.

"What's that for?" I asked.

"We bet each other it would be a black family," Bruce said.

We laughed. "Remember the Carters?" Carl asked. "I swear the block smelled like fried chicken for weeks after they left."

"What I want to know is," I said, "how in the hell did they afford that house?"

"He's probably some kind of athlete," Bruce said.

"Or a rapper," Carl chimed in.

That house, the Johnsons' new home, had been on the market for almost two years. It was a large multi-million dollar home and the best on the block. It was an odd fit for our cul-de-sac. The previous owners were some hot-shot producer and his young, siliconed wife. It was a modest house when they moved in, not too much different than my own. Now it had pillars and columns and solid gold handles on frosted glass doors. It was tall and glaringly white with a second-story deck that wrapped around the whole floor. The producer and his wife

had only lived there for as long as it took them to finish renovating
before they got divorced and put it on the market.

Now some black guy was living there.

"Who cares how they afforded it?" Steve said. "Let's just talk
about the party."

The Johnson Family Welcoming Party was scheduled for the
following Saturday. We wrapped up around ten and I locked up
behind Steve, always the last to leave. I turned off all the lights and
made my way upstairs, stopping to look in on each of my children.
Sam and Sabrina shared a room at the top of the stairs. They were both
tucked into their twin beds, Sabrina holding her doll and Sam holding
tightly to a book. Theo was in the room next door and, as I expected,
wide awake. He was sitting on his bed flipping through a magazine.
The television was on and once again those headphones were stuck to
his head and he was bopping hard to whatever he was listening to.
When he saw me, he took them off and smiled.

"Wassup, Dad?" he asked.

I grinned at him from the doorway and came into the room,
standing at the foot of the bed. "How is it possible, son, that you can
listen to music, watch television and read a magazine all at the same
time?"

He thought about it for a moment and said, "I don't know. I guess I'm just good that way."

"Well, pick one and turn it off," I said. Then I looked down at the magazine he was reading. There was a black girl in a pink bikini on the glossy pages. Her back was turned to the camera while she looked over her shoulder with her bright red lips parted, her pink tongue poking out to wet them. She was squatting down, her dark skin glistening. Her ass was grotesquely fat and seemed larger then life. I frowned but chose not to comment.

"Good night, son."

I left his room and joined Carolyn in our bedroom where she was twisted in some odd yoga position on the floor. One good thing about Carolyn was that she'd stayed in shape after we got married. Bruce and Carl always told me how lucky I was that my wife was still gorgeous after nineteen years.

I began to undress. "We're going to have a party for the Johnsons on Saturday. I told the guys I'd be in charge of food so would you run to the market and pick up the things on the list?"

She didn't even glance my way as she got up from the floor and moved to the closet behind me. "Anything else?"

I crawled into bed and reached for my book. "Yes. Fry some chicken and make a couple of those lemon tart things."

She whipped around. "You want me to buy all the food for this party and cook it too?"

"Is that a problem?"

"Yes, it's a problem, Dave. You won't even let me help plan these things and then you make up a chaotic list of things to do that never get done."

"The guys and I have it all straight," I said. "Don't worry about it. Just do what I asked you."

"Fine," she said, throwing up her hands.

"And when you go in the shower would you try wiping it out when you're done? Last time you left hair all over the walls."

She stood there for a moment, glowering at me. Then she went into the bathroom and slammed the door behind her.

***

That Saturday was hotter than hell. We got started early in the morning, putting up streamers and stringing a Welcome sign from the trees on my property. Theo helped Carl and I set up the barbecue pit and get the speakers situated. The few kids who lived on the block had started a game of street hockey. Sabrina and Sam had dragged their wading pool out and were filling it with water and toys, splashing each other in the process and laughing hysterically.

"Dad, what is this?" Theo asked. He held up some CDs I'd brought out.

"Uh, Pink Floyd, Garth Brooks, and Bruce Springsteen."

"You for real?"

"About what? Hey, go see if your mother is done with that fried chicken."

"You gotta change this music, Dad," he said as he went inside.

"Daddy!" Sabrina cried out. "Sam is throwing up in the pool!"

My son was leaning over the edge of the pool, coughing and puking his guts out. The water was polluted with floating bits of food. "Shit. Carolyn! Carolyn!"

She came out of the house. "What is it?" she snapped.

I pointed down at Sam and she picked him up and took him inside. Theo came back out and handed me a CD book. "Pick something from here. But don't play that stuff you had."

"What's wrong with my music? We've never had complaints before."

He made a face and said, "Those were white people, Dad. Ty and Ronda don't listen to the same kind of music you do."

"Whoa, whoa," I said, stopping him before he could walk away. "Ty and Ronda? When did you meet them?"

"When they moved in," he said. "I helped them unload their stuff."

Theo went to the stereo and pulled up a chair. He put a CD in and turned the volume way up. After the first ten or so swears, Carl and Bruce came over to me and said, "What is this?"

"Their kind of music," I said, nodding toward the Johnsons' house.

"So where are they?" Bruce asked, glancing across the street. "Nobody's been outta there all day."

I noticed that too but didn't think much of it. I put Theo in charge of the grill and Carl, Bruce and I walked across the street to their house. We rang the bell at least twenty times but got no answer.

"You gotta be kidding me," I said.

Bruce went to a window and peered in. "Looks like nobody's home."

I pushed the bell again. Still no answer. "Apparently not."

I was livid. After all we went through to plan this party, after going out of my way to welcome those people to our block and extend some neighborly hospitality, they don't even have the courtesy to show up. The three of us went back across the street and I shut off that stupid rap crap and put my Springsteen on. Screw it.

While we were cleaning up later that night, Carolyn said, "I can't believe they would just not show up. Are you sure you even told them about it?"

"I'm not an idiot, Carolyn," I snapped. "Of course I told them."

"Then why didn't they show?" she said. "When I spoke with Ronda she seemed so excited about the whole thing."

I paused. "Wait. You met them too?"

She shrugged. "I ran into her at the market last week."

"How'd you know it was her?"

"Well, there aren't that many black people in Whispering Gardens are there?" she snapped.

"No, and that's probably for a reason."

"She happened to be a very nice, well-educated woman."

"I don't care how nice they are," I said, scraping potato salad into the garbage. "What they did was rude. What kind of people would do something like that?"

Carolyn sighed. "Don't you think you're getting a little too worked up over this?"

"No," I said. "No, I don't. I put a lot of hard work into this."

"Oh right," she said, peeling off the yellow rubber gloves she was washing the dishes with. "That was you picking up one hundred and seventy dollars worth of food and frying five pounds of chicken that no one even ate."

"Don't start with me, Carolyn."

"You don't have to worry about that." She stomped out of the kitchen.

On Monday morning as I was leaving to go to work, I saw Tyrone in his driveway washing a Mercedes. The morning sun was shining off the silver hood as he ran his cloth over it. I looked down at my Nissan and noticed for the first time that the paint had dulled and mud had splashed up onto the sides.

I thought about going over there and giving him a piece of my mind and decided it wouldn't be a bad idea. I tossed my briefcase in the backseat and crossed over.

"Morning, pal," I said as I approached him.

"How's it going, Dave?" He picked up the hose and turned it toward the tires.

"All right. I was just on my way to work. Say, what happened to you guys on Saturday?"

Tyrone frowned a little. "Nothing. We took the kids to the amusement park."

"Okay," I said. "We had the party for you guys this weekend. On Saturday."

He paused for a second. "Damn man, we forgot. Ronda told
me something about it but I didn't remember whether it was this
Saturday or next. How was it?"

I shrugged. "It was all right. Lots of leftover food."

He only nodded and continued washing his car. It became
clear he wasn't going to apologize for inconveniencing the whole block.
I said good bye and went back to my car.

When I arrived home later that day, my whole block was filled
with cars. Someone had left a blue Cadillac haphazardly parked on the
curb, the tail end blocking my driveway. Loud music was thumping
and clouds of gray smoke rolled up into the air. And all of this was
coming from the Johnsons' backyard. Martin and Sara Reid, who lived
right next door to the Johnsons, came out the front door with
aluminum-covered plates, smiling and waving to a black woman in a
purple swimsuit who was standing in the doorway. The Shepherds,
who lived about two houses over from me, went into the backyard in
their swimsuits.

My house was empty. The television was still playing and
someone had left the back door open. I went upstairs to change and
watched out the window as people double-parked and went into the
Johnsons' yard. What the hell was going on?

My curiosity got the best of me so I crossed the street and rang

the doorbell of the Johnsons' house. That same black woman in the

purple swimsuit answered and smiled. "Can I help you?"

"I'm Dave from across the street."

"Oh, right. Ty was telling me about you. I'm his wife, Ronda."

She stepped aside and motioned me in. "Everybody's in the back and

there's beer and hamburgers in the kitchen. Don't be afraid to help

yourself."

"Thanks," I said.

The house was just as decadent and lavish as I'd always

imagined it to be. Marble floors and high ceilings, Italian leather

furniture, a fish tank the size of my bathtub in the living room wall and

a kitchen that looked bigger than my whole house. They had art on the

walls along the hall that came to an end with a wall of glass doors

leading out to the yard.

This house had the best view of the valley. The sun was

sinking into the trees and the breeze was light and cool. As I stepped

out into the yard, I nearly choked when I saw the cascading waterfall

and the TWO hot tubs full of people. Sam and Sabrina came zipping

down a slide I hadn't even seen, crashing into the pool behind three

little black kids. My wife was snuggled between two big black guys and Steve in one of the hot tubs. When she saw me standing there, livid, she got out and came over to me.

"Hey," she said, wringing out her long blond hair. "You got my note?"

"No." I looked around at the mix of people, some from the block, the rest obviously friends or relatives of Ty and Ronda. "What the hell is going on?"

"Ty and Ronda felt bad about missing the party so they threw one and invited everyone over."

"How come no one told me?"

"It was an impromptu get-together," she said. "Come meet Ty's cousins. They're the nicest guys and so smart."

I shook my head and pushed her hand away from my arm. "I'm going back home."

"Dave, don't be like that. They didn't do it to hurt your feelings."

"My feelings aren't hurt," I said. "Have fun."

When I got back home, I filled a cooler with beers and took out a steak to throw on the grill. I had just finished a beer when Bruce tapped on the gate and came in.

"How's it going, buddy?" he asked.

"Peachy."

He took a beer and sat down on top of the cooler. "Did you go to the party over there?"

"I dropped in for a second," I said. "Not really my scene."

He nodded. "I know what you mean." He swigged his beer. "Can you believe those guys?"

"No!" I shouted. "All that trouble we went to and they go and throw their own party. Talk about lack of etiquette."

"I know," he said. "I'm so pissed. Judy's like, 'You're just being a baby about it'. But we went to a lot of trouble."

"Right," I said, relieved that someone finally understood. "I'm so pissed."

"Yeah."

For a while we just sat there drinking our beers and being pissed. Then Bruce said, "Hey, you know what we should do? We should get together a bunch of the guys and play poker on Thursday."

"That'd be fun," I remarked absently.

"Yeah. We should invite Ty. Maybe we could win back some of the money we spent on that party that never was."

I paused and turned to look at him. "You know what? That's a damn good idea, Bruce."

We spread the word around the neighborhood that there would be a men's only poker game at Bruce's on Thursday night. I called Tyrone later that evening to ask him if he'd like to join us.

"Hey, Dave. How's it going? Didn't see you at the party this afternoon."

"Yeah, I had other things to do," I replied sarcastically.

He only laughed and said, "What can I help you with?"

"Well, the guys want to get together and play poker on Thursday and we'd like for you to join us."

"Sure, yeah," he said. "I ain't played poker in a while."

"Great," I said. "Come loaded because we really get into our games."

"You ain't saying nothing but a word, Dave."

"Um, okay. See ya then, pal."

Around sunset, I found Carolyn out front planting flowers in the bed. She'd changed out of her swimsuit into a pair of cut-offs and a t-shirt. I sat on the stoop and watched her for a few minutes. Living in this house with her these last few years had been like walking a tightrope twenty-four hours a day. I couldn't say this because it hurt her feelings. I couldn't do that because it was inconsiderate and so on. I had some vacation time coming up that I wanted to use. Maybe I'd take a nice trip out to Yellowstone. Alone.

"Have a nice time?" I asked.

"I sure did."

"Where'd you get the flowers?"

"Rhonda. She owns a couple of nurseries."

"Where are the kids?"

She pointed across the street to the Johnsons' front yard. Sabrina came running out of the backyard, one of Tyrone's sons in hot pursuit. He tackled her on the lawn and straddled her, pinning her arms over her head. I jumped up and ran across the street, yanking the boy off my baby daughter.

"Yo, get off me," the boy said, wriggling in my arms.

"Sabrina, get up!" I shouted.

"Daddy, we was just playin'," she said.

"You'd better clean up that language, young lady. Get across the street." She ran over to her mother. I let go of Tyrone's son and he ran away. Then Theo came out of the backyard with a girl wearing next to nothing. I glared at them as they approached me and saw Theo's fingers intertwined with hers.

"Wassup, dad," he said. "This is Ty's niece, Shakira."

"Nice to meet--"

"Theo, it's time to go home."

He frowned at me. "Dad, I was just gonna chill here for a while. Is that okay?"

"No, it isn't. Get home now." He did as I said but not before kissing Sharika or Shanika or whatever the hell her name was on her cheek.

"Dave," Carolyn said to me when I came back across the street. "Why did you do that? Sam and Sabrina like playing with Kevin and Amir."

"He was being rough with her," I said. "And the way they're talking these days...I just can't tolerate that."

"You're being ridiculous," she hissed.

"Don't tell me what I'm being," I shouted. "I'm right. Let them keep hanging around over there and you'll see. They've already got Theo!"

"I can't even look at you right now," she said, pushing past me to enter the house.

"That's because I'm right!"

The following morning, I waved to Rhonda as she ushered the kids into the car. She only stared at me before getting in her car and driving off.

Thursday evening came and I crossed the street to Bruce's for the poker game. I saw Tyrone as he left his house. He fell into step beside me as we walked down the block.

"How's it going, pal?" I asked.

"Good," he said, staring down at the pavement as we walked. "My son said you grabbed him the other day while he was playing with your daughter."

"Oh. I just, uh, I just felt that he was being a little too rough with her. She's a girl, after all."

He stopped and looked me in the eyes. "And my niece said that she tried to introduce herself to you and you were rude. She said you barely looked at her."

I chuckled. "Well, she was dressed a little inappropriately."

"That's your opinion. Pal."

We were greeted at the door by Bruce's wife, Judy. "Hi, Dave," she said. She turned to Ty and spread her arms wide for a hug. "How are you, Ty? How did Rhonda like the gym?

"Oh, she loved it," he grinned, accepting the hug. "Now she wants me to join with her. Thanks a lot, Judy."

Judy bared her large teeth and laughed. "It was my pleasure. The guys are in the kitchen and there's lots of beer. By the way, thanks for telling me about that discount market in Cedarville."

"Ya'll pay too much money around here for stuff," he said, as we came into the house. "The cheaper stuff is just as good as the expensive stuff."

"Something you learned in the 'hood?" I asked jokingly.

Ty looked at me like I'd just pissed on his leg. We went into the smoky kitchen and joined Steve, Carl and Bruce at the table.

"Well, it's about time you guys showed up," Bruce said, chomping down on his cigar. "We were about to send out a search party. Pick up your cards, fellas."

I sat across from Ty at the table and every now and again, I'd catch him staring at me. What bothered me most about the staring was that when I looked at him, he didn't look away.

As the night progressed, everyone loosened up. He smoked a cigar and drank beer and talked with Steve and Carl about basketball.

"You ever play basketball, Tyrone?" Bruce asked.

He looked at Bruce and said, "Why do you ask that? Because I'm black?"

Bruce stammered, "N-no, no. Not at all. I was just wondering."

Tyrone burst into laughter. "I'm just messing around with you, Bruce. I love sports. I'm just not too good at them."

"Me either," Steve said. "Two left feet and all elbows."

They laughed together over that. I gave Steve a look that he ignored.

"So you've all been here for a long time, huh?" he asked us.

I said, "Bruce, Carl and I have lived here for about twelve years. Steve's been here for about five."

He nodded. "Okay. It's cool that ya'll hang out. My old neighborhood wasn't like this."

"Where was that?" I asked.

"Beverly Hills."

All of us exchanged looks.

"What do you do, Ty?" I asked. "If you don't mind me asking."

"Not all at," he said and beamed proudly. "My wife and I are both entrepreneurs. Rhonda owns several nurseries and I own Victory Sports and Athletics."

"Holy shit!" Steve exclaimed. "You own Victory? That's like one of the biggest sporting goods chains in the US. I bought my softball team equipment from there!"

"No wonder you could afford to live in this neighborhood," I mumbled.

Everyone stared at me. Tyrone only chuckled and scratched his chin, that garish gold bracelet twinkling in the lamp light. "Okay."

"I call," Steve said, throwing some chips onto the pile.

"Me too," said Bruce.

"And me," came Carl.

"What you got fellas?" Tyrone asked, a greedy grin on those thick pink lips.

They laid their hands out and groaned collectively. I held onto mine, waiting for Ty.

"Dave?" he said to me.

"After you, my friend."

"I'm not your friend. But I insist."

I laid my cards out, confident with my three of a kind. I swear I could have smashed his face in when he laughed and laid down that straight flush. He swept the whole pile of chips over to him and got up from the table. "It's been real, fellas."

"Don't you wanna collect your money?" Steve asked.

He looked right at me and said, "Don't need it." He tossed three hundred dollar bills on the table and said, "Hope that covers the party." Then he left.

When I got home, Carolyn was standing on the front porch talking to some black guy. When I got closer, I realized it was one of the guys she had cozied up to in the hot tub at Ty's party.

"Carolyn."

"Yes, Dave?" she asked petulantly.

The guy and I looked at each other. He towered over me by a foot but I wasn't intimidated. All these guys think they can use their muscles to scare people. I wasn't afraid of him and I wanted my look to show him I wasn't. I went inside the house.

When she came up a while later, I said, "Who was that?"

She took off her clothes and pulled her nightgown on. "Ty's cousin, Bret. He was at the party."

"Sorry, I wasn't invited."

She stared at me for a moment. "What's your problem?"

"Right now, it's you."

She actually looked shocked. "Me? What did I do?"

"What were you doing talking to that ni—guy anyway? Since when do you like black guys?"

She angrily pulled a brush through her hair and tied it up. "I had no idea you were so narrow-minded."

"Oh please," I said. "This isn't about me being narrow-minded. You just wanna piss me off because you're still mad over Saturday."

"No, maybe you're the one who's still mad over Saturday. Don't take it out on me."

"You are pushing me so hard, Carolyn. Don't."

She said nothing more as she climbed into bed. As she was switching off the lamp, she said, "Maybe if you weren't so hostile all the time, I'd talk to you instead of him."

I came out of my house early on Saturday morning and saw Ty sitting atop a John Deere, leisurely circling his lawn. I thought about the poker game and that arrogant look he gave me before slapping down those hundred dollar bills. The nerve of that bastard. I guess he should be proud that someone like him could make that sort of money. Ever since he moved onto this block, he's been walking around like the king of Whispering Gardens. And these idiots on the block were just eating it up, laughing and joking with him like it was okay. Well, I wasn't about to pretend that I liked him or even wanted him here anymore.

I crossed over to his side of the street. He shut the mower off and waited for me to say something.

"We seem to be having some difficulties," I said.

He only nodded and said, "Yeah."

"Well, I think we should do something about it. See, this is a good neighborhood and I don't want anything or anyone messing that up."

"So what are you saying, pal?"

The way he said pal caused a tiny spasm in my chest. My palms started to sweat. "I'm saying, buddy, that we need to talk about the problem we're having."

"I'm not having a problem," he said, rising from the mower. "You're the one with the problem."

"And what problem is that?"

"You're a racist."

For a second, I was too shocked to say anything. "I'm not racist."

He waved his hand at me. "All right. If you insist."

"You're a real son of a bitch."

Tyrone laughed. "I bet you're dying to call me a nigger right now, aren't you?"

"If I wanted to, I would," I growled.

He spread his arms as if to say, "Come on and try it." My fists were clenched tightly and my heart was hammering away in my chest. I wanted nothing more than to punch this asshole's lights out. Who'd he think he was calling me a racist? Just because I didn't like him I was a racist? What a bunch of bull!

"You're not worth it," I snarled.

When I got back to my house, I called everyone into the living room.

"Wassup, Dad?" Theo asked, coming down the stairs. "Something wrong?"

I looked at him and his baggy jeans, tank top and big silver chain swinging around his neck. "Yeah, something's wrong. The way you're dressed. Go change."

"But this is what I like."

"I don't give a damn! Who paid for that stuff anyway? You, Carolyn?"

"What's the matter with you?" she demanded.

"That asshole across the street just called me a racist. From now on, nobody in this house is allowed over there. I don't want my kids anywhere near those negroids."

"Dave!" Carolyn shouted. "Do you even hear yourself?"

"Why are you saying that about Ty and Ronda, Dad?" Theo asked. "They're good people."

"How the hell do you know? You think because you dress like some black son of a bitch with his pants around his damn knees that you know them?"

His expression hardened and his eyes turned a shade of cold I'd never seen on his face before. He turned and ran up the stairs.

"I don't want my children over there again, Carolyn. I'm not kidding around."

They all stared at me like I was some three-headed monster. I
brushed by Carolyn and went out onto the patio. I paced to calm
myself down.

"Hey, pal." Bruce came through the back gate. "What's wrong?
You look pissed."

I could barely talk I was so mad. "That bastard across the
street...you know what he just said? He called me a racist."

"Are you kidding me?" Bruce shouted. "He's calling you a
racist? The nerve of that son of a bitch!"

"And Carolyn and the kids are all pissed at me. My own
family taking sides against me. This is unbelievable. It really is."

Bruce gave my back a slap and said, "You need to blow off
steam. Come on with me to Piper's. We'll have a few beers."

I had some time to cool down on the ride to Piper's Pub in
nearby Cedarville. Bruce and I sat at the bar with a few of our buddies
who were regulars there. I started drinking right away, sparing no time
for inane small talk. I didn't even want to talk about what had just
happened with Bruce yet. What the hell was wrong with this country
when a man can't dislike whoever he wants without someone calling it
racism? If I were so much of a damn racist, I would have had that
darkie and his family out of this neighborhood before they could even
open the moving truck. But I didn't. I was willing to put up with them

in my neighborhood. I even let my kids in their house, exposing them to God only knows what kind of depravity. I'd say that was pretty damn generous of me. Even that goddamn party. Why would I do something like that for someone I hated?

If I had him right here in front of me, I'd tell him exactly how I felt — that he was arrogant asshole jerk who liked flashing his big bucks and thinking he was better than everyone.

I kept putting away beer after beer, still unable to wrap my head around the whole thing. I was getting sloppy drunk. But I didn't care if Carolyn would be mad because of it. And I didn't care if my kids hated me either. All I cared about was telling that son of a bitch exactly what I thought of him and his family.

"Can you believe this?" I said to Bruce after a while. The bar had almost emptied. "Screw it."

Bruce nodded and said, "Come on, buddy. We'll get you home before you can't walk anymore."

I stood up none too steadily and feel against the bar. "I'm not ready to go home yet. I'm still pissed. Asshole moves into *my* neighborhood, corrupts *my* family, and then calls *me* a racist!"

Bruce got up and came over to pull me up. "All right, buddy. We're going home."

"Fine," I said. "Take me home so everybody can sit around frowning and calling me a bastard under their breaths. Sure. Take me home."

Bruce drove us back home. Whispering Gardens was dark. There was only one streetlight at the corner of the cul-de-sac, washing the houses near it in golden orange. The rest of the block looked as though it had been swallowed into oblivion. Bruce pulled into his driveway and came around to help me as I spilled out of the car.

"You're a good friend, Bruce," I said. "You're with me right? You know that black bastard is a piece of shit, don't you? Don't you, Bruce?"

"Sure, buddy," he said but he didn't sound like it.

"Hold on." I stopped and straightened up. "I gotta pee."

"We're almost to your house. It's right there."

I shook my head and stumbled toward some bushes, alcohol sloshing around in my belly like liquid fire. "Can't hold it, man. I gotta go."

"Dave," Bruce said. "Come on, man. Don't do that. Dave!"

I unzipped and let it go. I even aimed upward and got some on the side of someone's house. Whose house was this anyway?

"Dave! Would you come on?"

The porch lights nearly blinded me. I stumbled back.

"What the--"

"Oh shit," was all I heard Bruce say before he ran off. I just stood there, my dick still out and pissing. Tyrone looked at me, looked at my dick, looked at me again and I knew he was going to kick the shit out of me.

"Hey," I said, backing away. "I'm sorry. I'm really drunk."

"What the fuck you think you doing? You pissed on my house?!"

"I'm--"

I barely saw his fist coming before he laid me out. I felt like I had just been smacked in the mouth with a bag of bricks. The porch lights went out and I was left alone, lying in the street.

***

I could hardly lift my head the next morning. There was an overturned bottle of Advil on the dresser and a bucket filled with pink puke beside the bed. I couldn't stop moaning as I crawled from beneath the sheets and went to the bathroom. I flinched at my haggard reflection. Tyrone had popped my lip like a water balloon with that punch. I tried to wipe the dried blood from my chin but it hurt like crazy. I gave up and went downstairs.

Carolyn and the kids were sitting around the table eating. No one said anything when I walked in. I sat down and worked some toast down my throat while I sipped coffee.

Theo turned his headphones up and slumped down in his chair. I frowned at him. "Sit up straight and turn that down."

He got up and walked out of the room. Shouting at him would have hurt more than silence, so I said nothing and kept trying to eat. Sam and Sabrina got up too and went out to play. Carolyn sat quietly and sipped her coffee.

"You not speaking to me either?" I asked her.

"What would you like me to say to you, Dave? I'm sure you don't want to hear what I really *want* to say."

"Fine. Be a bitch."

I got up and went outside. Sam and Sabrina were on the other side of the hedges, staring at something on the side of the house.

"What are you doing?" I asked them.

They looked at me and at each other before running off. I came around and looked at the splatter that was on the house. I stared at it for a good while before I realized what it was. Then I crossed the street and banged on his door. He took his sweet time coming and stared at me like I was the asshole.

"You threw shit at my house."

He looked over my shoulder, smiled and said, "I don't know what you're talking about."

"You know damn well what I'm talking about!" I roared. "This is really low."

"So it's okay for you to come piss on my house but when the shoe's on the other foot, it's a problem? That's white people for you."

"What the hell does that mean?"

He sighed. "You'll have to excuse me. My family is having breakfast." He slammed the door in my face.

I practically ripped the goddamn door of the hinges when I went home. I paced around the living room, cursing and kicking things out of my way. And when I calmed down a little, I called a N.U.G. meeting.

"What's this about?" Carl asked as he and Steve took a seat on the patio.

"Just shut up a minute," I snapped.

Carl frowned and said, "No need to get that way, Dave. I was just asking."

Bruce came through the back gate. "What's going on?"

"We're having a meeting," I said.

"About what?" Steve asked.

I pointed across the way. "The Johnsons have got to go."

Nobody said anything for a long while. Finally Carl said, "Why?"

"Because," I shouted. "This neighborhood isn't safe anymore. Not with them running around."

"Yeah, but why?" Steve asked. "They seem to be doing all right."

"Oh yeah? Well, how do you explain me waking up to find shit splattered all over the side of my house! Huh? Can you?"

Carl and Steve had to hold back laughter and that pissed me off. Then Bruce says, "Well, Dave, you did piss on the front of his house."

"You pissed on his house?" Steve exclaimed. "What the hell is the matter with you, Dave? Are you nuts?"

"No, I'm not nuts! *I'm* fine. *They* are the ones who are nuts!"

"Because *you* pissed on *their* house," Steve said sardonically.

I was getting sick of Steve and his attitude. "One more word out of you and you're out of N.U.G. for good."

He got up and said, "Like I give a crap." Then he left.

"Fine!" I shouted after him. "Anybody else wants to go too?" I looked at Bruce and Carl. "You guys feel that way too?"

"You need to relax, man," Bruce said, shaking his head.

"Don't tell me to relax! This bastard is ruining our neighborhood and I'm sick of it. I'm not putting up with this crap anymore! Are you guys with me?"

I knew Bruce would take my side. Carl looked like he was still on the fence.

"Carl? You with us? Come on. You remember how much you hated the Carters? You were dancing a friggin' jig when they moved."

"Yeah," he said, "but it wasn't because they were black."

"And neither is this," I said. "They just don't belong in this neighborhood."

Both of them sat there quietly for a while. Then Bruce says, "So, what? Are we gonna just *ask* them to leave?"

I started to pace. "No. That's not going to work. He won't leave without a fight. We need to do something to make them want to leave."

Carl sighed and ran his hand down his face. "I can't believe I'm doing this."

"What? We're not killing anybody. We're just doing what we have to do to keep the neighborhood peaceful. Isn't that why we formed N.U.G. in the first place?"

Carl thought about that for a moment. "It has been kinda…chaotic since they moved in. Always blasting music and just hanging out on the lawn."

"And their guests are always blocking my driveway," Bruce said.

Then I got an idea. "I know what we can do."

I asked the guys to come back later that night for Operation Johnson Removal. Bruce and I had to wait for Carl and when he finally came out, his wife followed him. She screeched at him halfway down the block until she turned around and went back to the house.

"Let's just get this done so I can get back home," Carl sighed.

"What's with Linda?" Bruce asked him.

He shrugged. "The usual."

"Okay, look," I said. "This is what we're going to do."

I went to the trunk of my car and took out a bag. I handed it off to Bruce. He looked inside and frowned and passed it to Carl who had the same reaction.

"This is vandalism, Dave," Carl said. "I said I didn't want to do anything illegal."

"We'll blame it on those kids from around the block. Carl, would you quit worrying?"

He pulled his hand roughly down his face and sighed, "I can't believe I'm doing this."

Each of us armed ourselves with spray cans and crossed the street. Ronda's car sat in the driveway. Tyrone's car was gone and the porch lights were out. Bruce said, "Doesn't look like anybody's home."

"Well we better be quick," I said.

We started spraying the hell out of Ronda's car and the white gate to the backyard. Bruce sprayed the manicured lawn until the entire thing looked black. I felt vindicated but not nearly enough. This asshole threw shit at my house. I wanted him to see that that kind of behavior just wouldn't be tolerated. So I decided to spray a little message on the front of his house to drive my point home even further.

"What are you doing?" Carl asked when he saw me spraying.

"Leaving a little note," I said.

"Dave, you're taking this too far," Bruce said. "Let's go home."

"Almost done." I finished the last letter just as a car turned down the block. "Shit! Let's get out of here."

We hid in the Reids' bushes as the car came down the block. They parked on the street and got out of the car. I held my breath as they walked across the lawn. Tyrone had his arm around Ronda as she held one of their sons who was fast asleep in her arms. The other held Tyrone's hand as they went inside.

Carl breathed a big sigh and started walking home. "Good night, guys."

Bruce and I crossed the street and went into the garage. I offered him a beer but he shook his head. "I wonder what's with Carl," I said. I took a swig of beer and laughed. "I can't wait to see that bastard's face tomorrow when he sees what we did."

Bruce was quiet for a minute. "Yeah." Then he got up and said, "I'm gonna take it down, buddy. Catch you tomorrow."

I locked up after Bruce and went to the bathroom. There were black specks all over my hands and forearms from the spray paint. I must have stood at the sink scrubbing my hands for an hour and it wouldn't come off. After a while I gave up and went up to bed.

***

The doorbell rang as I was grabbing my briefcase the following morning. My heart nearly jumped into my throat when I opened it and a cop was standing there.

"Morning, officer," I said casually. I even smiled. "Can I help you with something?"

"Maybe," he said very seriously. "There was an act of vandalism committed on this block last night." He pointed over his shoulder and I saw the crudely drawn message: **GO BACK HOME NIGGERS!**

"What's going on?" Carolyn asked, coming to stand beside me. She gasped when she saw the writing. "Oh my god! Who would do something like that?"

"Probably some teenagers in the area," the officer said. "We found the spray cans in the neighbor's bushes."

"Jeez, that's terrible," I said. "The Johnsons are such nice people."

I felt Carolyn's eyes swing to me but she didn't say anything. "If we can do anything to help, officer..."

"Did either of you see anything? Hear any strange noises last night? Mr. Johnson thinks it was around eleven or so last night whiles he and his family were out."

Carolyn turned to me and said, "Weren't you out in the garage with Bruce and Carl last night?"

I thought if I said anything I'd incriminate myself so I just shrugged. The officer nodded and said, "It's all right, sir. If you think of anything, just give us a call down at the station."

"We will, officer," Carolyn said. She closed the door when he left. "God, I can't believe someone would write something so horrible. And in Whispering Gardens? What is this neighborhood coming to?"

I grabbed up my briefcase and made a break for the door. "Don't know. I'll see you later."

As I was getting into my car, Ty came out of his house. He looked at me and I looked at him and I swear he knew. And he continued to watch me, even after I got in the car and zoomed down the block.

When I got home that afternoon, news vans were parked on the block. Men in white coveralls were painting over the graffiti on Ty's house. Ronda's car was being towed away. Ty was standing on his porch speaking with a reporter. Because things like this normally didn't happen in Whispering Gardens, the neighborhood had come out to watch. I saw Carl and Linda in the crowd and went over to them.

"What's going on here?"

"Someone vandalized the Johnsons' house with racist graffiti," Linda said. "Isn't that a shame?"

"Yeah," I said. "That's terrible."

"The cops think it was someone on the block," Carl said.

"I just hope they catch them," I sighed. "We can't have this neighborhood turning into a circus."

Linda nodded her agreement but Carl just stared at me. I said good bye to them and crossed over to my house. Theo and Carolyn were in the kitchen talking. They stopped when I came in but neither spoke to me.

"Hello to you too," I said, going to the fridge for a beer.

"Theo, I want to talk to your father," Carolyn said.

"Okay," he said. He gave me a look before passing by.

"What's with you?" I asked, sitting across from her at the table.

"Did you do it, Dave?"

"Do what?"

"Don't play dumb, Dave. Did you spray that racist graffiti on the Johnsons' house?"

I sighed. "What if I did?"

She snorted with disgust. "I knew it."

"I didn't confess anything," I said.

"You don't have to," she said. "It's all over your hands."

I looked down at the black specks.

"This is not working anymore, Dave. I can't take you and your temper anymore. You're nothing like the man I thought I married. You keep turning more and more into an ogre every day."

"Oh, give me a break would you? All this melodrama was cute when we were dating but now it's just old. Let's drop this, all right. I want my dinner."

She stood up and very calmly said, "Fuck you and your dinner," and walked out of the kitchen.

I tossed my beer and was about to follow her upstairs when the doorbell rang. It was the same officer who'd come to the door earlier.

"Sir, can you step outside for a moment?"

My eyes immediately went across the street where I saw a squad car parked in front of Carl's house.

"What's this about, officer?"

"Sir, please."

My eyes kept darting from Ty's house to the officer. They knew. They wouldn't be here otherwise. I stepped outside and extended my hands toward the officer.

"What can you tell me about your neighbor, Carl Thayer?"

I dropped my hands. "He's a good guy," I said, a little confused. "He's married, has four daughters, owns a paint business."

The officer wrote something on a pad. "And you were with him last night?"

I nodded reluctantly. "Yeah for about an hour. Maybe less."

"Do you know what Mr. Thayer did after leaving you last night?"

"As far as I know he went straight home."

The officer nodded and said, "Thank you, sir. Have a good one."

"Yeah."

When I came back inside, Carolyn was pulling a suitcase behind her down the stairs. The kids followed her, each of them carrying an overnight bag.

"What is this?" I demanded.

Carolyn brushed hair from her face. "Kids, tell your father you love him and that you'll see him later."

Sam and Sabrina gave me a quick hug and stepped back. Theo just stood there, staring down at his sneakers.

"Carolyn—what the hell is going on? Where are you going?"

"Theo, please take your brother and sister to the car and wait for me."

I watched as he ushered them outside without a glance in my direction. "Carolyn, you better tell me what's going on or so help me--"

"You know, I'm really sick of you threatening me all the time, Dave. I'm your wife, not someone you can bully. I deserve your respect. And until I get it, the kids and I are going away for a while."

"You can't take the kids! Why are you doing this?"

"You did this."

She walked out and slammed the door behind her. I chased after her but froze halfway across the lawn when I saw the officer escorting Carl out to the squad car and assisting him in. Linda stood on the porch crying. Carolyn followed the car down the block.

"Linda!" I called. I ran over to her and asked, "What's going on? Did he just arrest Carl?"

She wiped tears from her eyes and made a scoffing noise. "Yes. They said he was the one who vandalized the Johnsons' house. The spray cans were from our store."

"Oh no."

"And they found his fingerprints on the can they recovered. Why would he do something like that, Dave? You know Carl. He's not that kind of man."

She fell on me and sobbed her eyes out. I couldn't say anything; I just patted her back and told her it would be okay. "No, it won't," she cried. "We're going to lose the business. We'll lose everything. Why didn't he think about us?"

After I left Linda, I went to Bruce's and banged on the back gate. "Bruce! Bruce, open up! We need to talk!"

Judy came to the gate and opened it. "Dave, Bruce isn't in the mood for company."

"I know, Judy. But I just need to talk to him for a few minutes."

She sighed and stepped aside to let me in. Bruce was sitting in his deck chair smoking a joint. He looked up at me, then rolled his eyes and turned his gaze back to the sky.

"I hope you know this is all your fault," he said calmly. He took a puff of the joint and stood up. "Carl's probably going to lose his business, I hope you know."

"Carl won't lose his business," I said, plopping down on a chair. "Where'd you get that? You don't smoke."

He shook his head, disgusted. "I can't believe we both just sat there and let you convince us that we needed to do this. They haven't even done anything. I mean, who cares if they listen to their music loud? Who cares if they hang out on their lawn? I just keep hearing myself saying over and over again, 'Their guests are always blocking my driveway.' What an asshole I was."

I sighed. "Would you give it a rest? We did what we did for a reason. Nothing's going to--"

"Yeah, we did. For your reason."

Judy came out onto the patio. She smacked her teeth and snatched the joint from Bruce. "Smoking yourself silly isn't going to solve anything, Bruce."

"I know, honey," he said. He sat down and covered his face with his hands. "I know."

"I think you should leave now, Dave," Judy said, glaring down at me.

"I'm still talking to--"

"Didn't you hear her?" Bruce snapped. "Go home, Dave."

I left Bruce's and crossed back to my house. As soon as I shut the door behind me, I went to the kitchen to grab a beer and tripped over one of Sam's trucks. I snatched it up and shouted up the stairs, "Sam! Get down here and get your damn toys out of people's way!"

There was no answer and suddenly I remembered that I was alone. She'd taken my kids and left me and I didn't know where they'd gone.

I tossed the toy aside and got my beer. I had just finished it and popped open another when the doorbell rang. Thinking it might be Carolyn and the kids, I ran to the door and pulled it open. I had a smile on my face, ready to forgive her for being such a drama queen, but that fell away the second I saw Tyrone's face in front of me.

"I guess I'm not who you were expecting."

He stepped past me and entered my house, looking around at everything. "You have a nice home, Dave. Kinda small though."

I just stared at him. "What do you want?"

He chuckled and said, "Shouldn't I be the one with the attitude? You and your buddies spray-painted the shit out of my house, ruined my wife's car that she worked hard for, called me and my family niggers and you're upset with *me*? That's a laugh, Dave."

My face was hot with anger. I couldn't remember ever feeling so much animosity for another person in my life. I hated Ty and I wanted him out of my life with a passion.

"You don't have any proof of anything. So why don't you get out of my house? Better yet, get off my block or you'll be sorry."

"No, you'll be the one who's sorry if you keep fucking with me, Dave," he said charging over to stand directly in front of me. "To you I'm just some ignorant nigger who you think you're better than. For what reason? 'Cause you're white? I can buy and sell your cracker ass a hundred times over. My wife and I probably have more education than you and your dumb-ass buddies put together."

"I'm sure you owe that to affirmative action and the benevolence of white people."

"I don't owe shit to you motherfuckers!" he shouted. "I work for mine while you get your life handed to you on a fucking platter. You don't own this block and I ain't your *boy*. And you're going to give me the respect I deserve."

I got right in his face and asked, "Or what?"

He smiled a little and stepped around me, slamming the door.

The next morning, I went over to Carl's house. Linda answered the door in her bathrobe, her eyes puffy and red.

"Can I help you, Dave?" she said very shortly.

"Um, I just wanted to know if Carl had come home yet," I said, confused by her attitude.

"Why?"

"I wanted to help you post his bail. Is something wrong, Linda?"

She snorted. "You have some nerve asking me that." Then she slammed the door in my face. As I was crossing back to my house, I saw the Reids in their driveway.

"Martin! Sara! Good morning!"

Both stared at me, said something to each other and got into their cars. I picked up the paper on my front lawn and took it inside. I stood on the other side of my door, trying to let go of the fear that had turned my stomach icy. Everyone knew. It was impossible for them not to know. But why would they believe him over me? I've known everyone on this block for at least twelve years.

I was just pouring myself a cup of coffee when I heard the sirens. I went to the window and peeked through the blinds. This time the squad car was parked in front of Bruce's house. My heart jumped into my throat when the front door opened and two uniformed officers led Bruce outside, his hands cuffed behind him. A cameraman followed them to the squad car while a photographer snapped away.

A sharp knock echoed through my house. I jumped and jostled my mug, spilling hot coffee on my hand. "Shit!"

"Mr. Coleman, open the door!"

My legs were ready to buckle. I could hear my heart pounding with every step I took toward the door.

"David Coleman?" one of the officers asked.

I nodded.

He motioned to his buddy. "David Coleman, you're under arrest…"

When I was released two days later, I came home to find Carolyn waiting in the driveway. It had been a long two days and I was weary. I had sat up in my cell the whole time, unable to sleep. When an officer came to the cell and told me that someone had posted my bond, I knew right away it was Carolyn. I also knew that she'd show up here. Maybe to make up, maybe to put the final nail in the coffin which had become our life together. As I got out of the taxi, she climbed out of her car and met me halfway across the lawn.

"You look terrible, Dave," she said, a slight smile on her face.

"If that's what you came here to say, you wasted a trip." I bypassed her and went into the house. She followed me inside. "Where are the kids?"

"With my sister. I didn't think it would be a good idea to bring them."

I snorted. "So much for you and your bright ideas."

A light in her face was extinguished. "I wanted to talk, Dave. Before I brought the kids back, before I came back. I wanted to know if this was worth saving."

I hadn't even realized how long it'd been since I'd looked my wife in the face. I always remembered her as the knockout babe I met in college. And she was still beautiful, still everything I'd always thought a wife should be. It wasn't enough to make me love her though. I sure wish I knew when that had changed. Maybe I had known all along.

"I think we both know the answer to that, Carolyn."

She started crying and I didn't even feel like comforting her. It shocked me that with all that was going on, I didn't even want her around. I turned away from her and started up the stairs but her voice stopped me.

"So we'll get a divorce then?" she said.

"Fine by me."

"I think you should know that Steve and I have feelings for each other."

I swung around. "What? Steve from next door? My *friend* Steve?"

"Yes," she said, sniffling. "We've always felt attracted to each other. But we never said anything until about two days ago."

My ears were roaring. "How could you? He's been in my house. Ate at my table. And you've been--"

"I've never had sex with Steve," she interrupted. "I just…you were always so cold to me. He was nice and sweet and funny. He treated me with respect, the way you were supposed to but never did."

"That's your excuse?" I said, disgusted. "That's all you have to say?"

"It's true!" she shouted. "You haven't touched me in months. I just don't love you, Dave. Good bye."

She practically ran for the door. I followed her, screaming, "I'm taking my kids away from you! You won't get away with this!"

The house rattled when I slammed the front door. I turned back and punched it, cracking and splintering the wood. I overturned the couch and threw framed photos of my children on the floor, sending the glass flying. I kicked the coffee table over and sent the end tables crashing against the staircase.

I fell back on the couch. I must have sat there for hours, just staring, not seeing anything. Finally my attention was caught by the blinking light of the answering machine at my feet. I reached down and pressed play.

"Hi, Dave. It's Martin," my boss's voice said. "I hate to do this over the phone but we have no choice but to let you go. Most of your clients have already requested someone else. The rest have left us. We appreciate your service over the years but your recent work performance and this scandal you're involved in is affecting our business. I'm sorry. We wish you all the b--"

I stopped the machine.

I pulled into the parking lot of Victory Sport and Athletics and cut the engine. It was an overcast day. For a while I just sat there, staring at the sign over the entrance. Then before I lost my nerve, I got out and went inside.

I asked a girl behind the register if Ty was around. She called his office and after speaking with him for a few minutes, pointed toward a door and told me it was his office. When I came in, he was standing behind his desk, his arms crossed over his chest. For a long while, we just stared at one another. Then I cleared my throat and said, "How's it going, buddy?"

He nodded. "Going great. And you?"

I shrugged. "As well as can be expected I guess."

He motioned me into the seat before his desk and he took his seat again. "What can I do for you, Dave?"

I laughed a little. "All right, we can get right to the point."

Ty wasn't amused. His cold expression hadn't changed since I walked in.

"You know, my life hasn't been all peaches and cream," I said. "I lost my job, my family... You aren't the only one who's had it rough."

"Am I supposed to feel sorry for you?"

I snorted. "I see you still want to be the victim."

"Oh no," he said. "You're doing a good job of that right now."

"What have you lost?" I snapped. "So some asshole called you a nasty name. You still have your business, your wife and kids are still there. I don't have a goddamn thing."

"Including your self-respect. If you'll excuse me, Dave, I have work to do." He stood up and went to open the door.

"All right, look," I said standing up too. "I didn't come here to open old wounds. I came because...I need a favor."

He laughed at me. "You're joking right?"

"No." I took a deep breath. "See, the thing of it is, my previous field is very competitive. You know, making room at the top for younger, brighter guys. And with the...you know... and my age, I'm

having a hard time finding work around here. I can barely afford the
apartment I'm staying in. So maybe you know someone…who needs
somebody."

Ty just stood there staring at me. After a few moments, he
closed the door to his office and sat down at his desk again. He rocked
back and forth, his fist pressed to his mouth.

"Hey, buddy. It's cool. You don't have to say anything." I got
up and started walking toward the door.

"Hold up, Dave." I turned back to him. "I do know somebody
who's looking for help."

"Yeah? Who?"

"A guy I know. You got any bookkeeping experience?"

"Five years."

He nodded. "I'll expect you here first thing Monday morning.
Wear office attire but we go casual on the weekends."

"Here?"

"Yes," he said. "Is that a problem?"

"No," I said. "Not at all. Thank you."

"I'm not doing you a favor, Dave," he said, opening a folder on
his desk. "I'm doing myself a favor. God will continue to be good to me
only if I can be good to my fellow man. Even after all you did to me
and my family, I can still find a place in my heart to forgive you."

"Well, I appreciate that," I said.

He looked up at me. "You should. I'll see you Monday."

But I didn't leave. I watched him type on his computer, pretending I wasn't there anymore. Then I said, "I came here to hurt you."

He paused and looked at me. I took the gun from my waistband and held it up for him to see. He stared at it but did not flinch or even show that he was afraid.

"I wanted to kill you," I said. "I wanted to walk in here, make you think I needed a job and when you rejected me, I was going to shoot you."

Tyrone pushed himself away from his desk and stood. He looked into my eyes as he raised his arms out at his sides. "So what stopped you?"

"I don't know," I said. "I guess you did."

"Don't quit on my account."

"You want me to do it?" I asked.

"Isn't that what you came here to do? 'Those niggers ruined my life. I had to shoot him, Officer.' Right?"

"This didn't start out being about race," I said.

"Then what was it, Dave?" He came around his desk and stood a few feet in front of me. "You need to be honest with yourself. You hated me on sight. You didn't want me and my family living on your block—not to mention the nicest house *on* your block. What did that say about you in your little fixer-upper that costs more than its worth?"

"Now you're trying to provoke me."

"Maybe I am," he said. "You stand here in front of me telling your sad little story like I'm supposed to excuse what you did? I don't want your excuses. What you did was evil and it was racist. Bottom line."

"I know what I did," I said, staring him straight in the eye. "Trust me, I know."

He snorted at me. "Get out of my office, Dave. I don't want to see you here again. If you show up, I'm calling the cops."

"Fine."

"One more thing," he called after me. I turned to face him. "Your wife was always talking about what a great guy you were. Kept telling me we would get along like gangbusters. Do you think she was right?"

I thought about it for a moment and shrugged. "We'll never know now, right?"

"Right."

I left his office. When I stepped outside it was raining. I covered my head and ran to my car.

The Upward Bound Negro

You are born as a black boy or a black girl.

You are born in the hood, the urban area, the ghetto. You are already perceived as having a slim chance of ever breaching the borders of a better place. You will probably not finish high school, get pregnant or get someone pregnant and never go to college. If you start liking hip hop too much and dressing in the hip-hop style, people will be afraid of you when they see you. If you can't break free of your hood colloquialisms and speak in proper English form, people will perceive you as ignorant and stupid. This is the measure of your fate.

You are the product of a single parent home. Your father left your mother but he still participates in your life. Your mother works hard at a job she does not like. You live in an apartment. You will live in many apartments throughout your life. Your neighborhood used to be clean and relatively safe. Your city used to be a booming metropolis. Those days have passed and now you live among abandoned homes, empty lots and cracked and broken sidewalks. You are too young to understand what poverty and racism has done to your community.

You attend school. You learn to read and write. You are praised for staying within the lines and reading with fluidity. You do what the teacher tells you, and even when you feel like misbehaving, you're still not punished as harshly as the other kids. Even at this young age, your teachers recognize your potential. You get many certificates and gold stars. You are gifted.

Success follows you throughout elementary school. You are a star pupil. You show signs of being a great leader. Growing up is a tight fit but you try to stick to doing your homework and not goofing off in class. Once or twice you get caught passing notes. Some teachers start to frown at you. You've disappointed them slightly by being so playful. But their smiles return when you score 100s on your tests.

High school will be hit or miss with you. Sometimes you will do remarkably well and other times you will founder. All you will really remember were the good times commingled with studying, tests and graduating pretty high in your class. Some of your recollections will bring a shudder as you recall that first awkward year of endless lunches alone, constant ridicule because your gear wasn't tight, or embarrassment from getting called on whilst unprepared. Still, in all high school was cool because it held the promise of two things: College and getting out of the city.

It is safe to assume that if you have gotten through taking the SATs, filling out college admissions applications, financial aid forms and participating in extracurricular activities that you are anxious to get out of the city and go forth into higher learning. There is nothing

wrong with wanting to leave the city. If you are hungry and there is no

food in the house, you would go someplace where there is food. Some

people are offended when they hear people say they want to get out of

a place. Especially if it is someplace that, to them, is quite cozy. They

are not really angry with you, they just don't understand where you

are coming from.

So now you've gotten into a college and you're leaving home,

probably for the first time. Your stomach is churning because you don't

know what to expect, particularly from the white kids because the only

thing you know about them is what you hear at home and what you

have learned in school. None of those things sit very well with you. But

you're not going to sweat it. You're not going to avoid them but if one

is cool, then you can be friends. For the time being, you'll just stick to

what you know.

You get to college, move in to your dorm and your roommate

is white. In fact, most of your suite mates are white and you're the only

person of color besides the Indian kid. They all seem to know one

another. But they seem cool and really interested in getting to know

you. They ask where you're from, if you had a girlfriend or boyfriend

back home. They ask if you want to come down and have dinner with

them in the caf. You accept.

Things are okay. Your classes aren't as tough as you heard they might be. You've made a few friends, mostly people of color, mostly from the same classes you take. But right now, your white roommates are the only ones you hang out with because they ask. You begin to notice stares here and there. Nothing big. Probably something you should just ignore. When you call home, you tell your mother that everything is fine and you need more money.

The first semester is a breeze. The second semester is more so. You remember all those times in high school when your teachers told you college was going to be hard and you laugh. What was so hard about it? You get your grades for the semester and you've nearly made the Dean's List. You and your friends of color look forward to spending the summer hanging out. Your white friends say good bye and hope that they see you again next year.

You've made the decision that you'll spend your sophomore year becoming more involved in student affairs at your school. For instance, you've noticed that some of the people of color don't have special interest groups. The white kids and the Asian kids (including the Pacific Islanders) have a wrap sheet full of activities. There are two Latino groups and one group for the black kids. But they aren't American black kids. They are African or West Indian kids and they have attitude when it comes to American black kids. You decide to

form a group with your friends. You present your idea and you're
rejected. There are too many clubs right now.

You and your friends are bitter because your club got rejected
while clubs for radical white feminists and Future Businessmen of
America stayed around. It is unfair. They don't represent the entire
student body, you think. Maybe you should have changed the name
from Black Unity Club to the more inconspicuous People's Unity Club.
Then you would have been accepted.

You go through the remainder of your sophomore year with
that dark cloud over your head. Your white roommates involved in
any clubs are subject to your scorn. Why do they always get what they
want? You and your friends ponder this all summer. You all start to see
that maybe some things aren't as liberal as people say.

In your junior year, you come back with a vengeance. Not only
are you going to try again to get your club approved, you're going to
take African American history courses. They don't count as major
credits toward your degree but you are interested, more so now than
you've ever been.

The words burn your eyes as they move across the page. Your
chest fills with emotions you are very familiar with but not on this
scale. This is something you've never read in your high school text
books. This is history you didn't know existed. How could this be?

Could it be true that your people lived this way, endured on this land after being kidnapped from their own? How could all of these people sit around you and be okay with knowing about the bloody past that still haunts people of color like an old ghost in the cellar? Maybe they just don't care because they don't feel they have to. It's not their history.

You start making calls home more frequently to tell your family everything you've learned. Nobody seems interested. Your mother only half-listens and tells you not to study too hard. But you don't think you've studied hard enough. As far as you're concerned, this is only the beginning. You start bracing yourself for what you will find out.

Nigger.

Something you used to say all the time. Maybe you didn't say nig*ger* but you've said nig*gah*. When you said it, you didn't mean it the way whites have historically used it. Even knowing that, you still feel guilty and tell yourself to stop saying it as of today. Still, you hear it slip out in conversation with your friends. When you're listening to your music, you don't hesitate to sing along to your lyrics. You notice your white roommate bopping his or her head, mouthing the words.

A fight breaks out in your suite. The Indian kid, Suresh, has punched one of your other suitemates in the mouth for impersonating

him as a convenience store clerk. "Thank you! Come again!" is
constantly shouted at him every time he leaves the suite. Suresh is
transferred to another suite, pending further action. You hear later that
Suresh has left the school.

One of your friends of color is being taunted by two white girls
in her English class. They point and laugh at her. One day your friend
is passed a note. It is a picture of a stick figure. The face is shaded in
with pencil and there is a noose tied around its neck. Your friend
doesn't report the incident.

The incident has pissed you off. It has also opened your eyes a
bit. It's not cool to let your suitemates say nigger, even if they are just
singing along to the music. You shouldn't say it around them either
because maybe they'll think its cool for them to say it. You talk to your
friends of color and ask them how many times they've felt they were
discriminated against on campus or how many times a white person
has said something racially offensive. You are surprised to hear how
many people have stories.

You try again to get your club approved and it's accepted.
Your school now has a Black Unity Club.

People sign up and come out to meetings. But meetings don't
go as you envisioned them. You wanted to sit around talking about
history, start some initiatives, protest and open the floor to friendly

debates. Everybody else just wants to chill out and play foosball. You can't compete against a Playstation and disinterested minds. You stop showing up to meetings of your own club. Later, you hear that it's become a club strictly for socializing.

Over the summer, you come to the decision that people don't care to know their history. They don't care enough to do anything about the discrimination they face. You can't understand why you care so much either. Your schoolwork for senior year has become more aggressive and complicated now that you are focused on your major and you really need to spend more time on that than anything else. Black empowerment can wait.

You graduate with a good ranking and a degree. Your mother is proud of you, your father is teary-eyed. You've made them both so happy. You will spend the summer hunting down a hot job and shopping for nice clothes to wear as you enter the real world. Your friends from school are looking around too but they don't feel too sure about themselves because they didn't secure internships. Your white roommates have all secured jobs at the top companies. Even the ones who rarely opened a book and spent all four years waking up from a perpetual hangover managed to get a decent suit and tie job.

You've relaxed up until July and then you hit the classifieds. You post your resume online and anxiously await hits. You get interviews. There you are in your professional attire, your hands folded in your lap, your posture better than it's ever been. And as you leave each place after each rejection, you vow to step your game up, have better answers, make more eye contact. Pretty soon, you'll land into your dream job.

You go for an interview at a place that you feel you are not really qualified for. But they've called you back so that is a good sign. You are cool and articulate throughout the interview. The woman interviewing you is white. She asks you a lot about your background. She says ain't. A lot. She comments on your outfit. She mispronounces your name and laughs. She's never heard that one before. What makes you a good candidate for this job? You have an answer for this. A good one. You believe in being a team player. You value hard work and can use your experience and education to bring innovative new ideas to the work. You also have a great personality conducive to a large office such as this one.

She does not seem impressed with your answer. She wraps the interview and does not accept the hand you offer to her. As the next candidate enters, you hear a change in her tone. You turn and see her firmly grasp the young white boy's or girl's hand before she closes the door.

It is nearing the end of September and your job hunt has not
been fruitful. You accept an entry level position at a company that has
nothing to do with why you went to school in the first place. It's in the
hood where you grew up. You've spent four years away, only to end
up back where you started.

Your boss is young and fired up. He or she likes efficiency so
he or she is always checking over your work and sending back
revisions on this and that. It may not have been what you wanted, but
you feel challenged and you believe you could do well here. Once you
have had adequate experience, you could move on to what you really
want to do.

You are not in the minority as a person of color but you notice
the separation in the cafeteria and even during break when people
come outside to smoke. Over time your belief that people of color
should unite has changed to *all* people uniting. Maybe that was what
part of what was wrong with the world now. You decide to make it a
point to mix with everyone.

When some of the other people of color notice you sitting
amongst the whites now, they shun you. Someone tries to undermine
your work in front of the boss. Someone else blames you for a mistake
that was made. You say what's up to someone in the hall and that
person looks away and keeps walking. You try to sit with them at the

lunch table but they don't speak to you. You go back to sitting with the white people.

They like you. You're funny. They are young like you and very interested in the city. They are from the suburbs, some from the Midwest. This is their first time living or working in the city. They ask you all sorts of questions. Have you ever been shot at? Have you ever seen a dead body? Do you know someone in jail? You laugh off some of their questions. Others you answer honestly. They like you even more. They think you are street smart and tough.

Some of them are hanging out at a bar and invite you to come along. You go. When you get to the bar you immediately notice that you are the only black person there. You order drinks and stay close to the people from work. They introduce you to everyone they know. Someone calls you their "black" friend. Someone else asks if you can get them weed. They laugh. Say they are kidding.

On Monday, your white friends talk about how much fun they had with you on Saturday. Pretty soon the whole office knows that you have been hanging out with them. You get invited to parties and more bars. The people of color don't have much to say to you beyond work stuff. The more you hang out with the white people, the more fun you have. You're used to their jokes by now and are sure they mean nothing by them. They become your full-time friends.

They ask you why the other black people in the office are not friendly. They ask why black people in general aren't friendly. They ask if you can wash your hair with regular shampoo and how you brush it. If you have light eyes or fine hair, they want to know how you got it. You start to feel like an animal in a zoo around them. They are fascinated with your sameness and differences.

You overhear two of the higher-ups chatting. A person of color in the office has asked for a very big assignment. They are debating if this person should have it. They are leaning towards another candidate. One of them asks if they think the person of color will be able to handle speaking with international clients. The other laughs and says only if they have Ebonics in China.

There is an office meeting. The boss calls attention to the language some of you use around the office. It is not professional, he says. When he speaks, he points at different persons of color. At lunch, a few of the people of color gather to talk about the meeting. The word racist is used several times. Everyone is upset. They've been denied assignments, turned down for raises. The boss is condescending when he addresses them. He calls one person of color by another person of color's name. When he is corrected, he waves his hand and asks, "What's the difference?"

Complaints have been filed. They have been ignored. People have quit. Still you sit at your desk, complete your assignments and try not to make a lot of noise. Yes, you are angry too. You have witnessed some of the treatment. But you are afraid of the majority. In their eyes, you are complaining for nothing. You are playing the race card. Every injustice you face is because of your skin color. Slavery is over, they say. You need to move on.

Your white friends are glad that you're not like "them". You don't act like the ones who are always complaining. You do your work and you don't blame "The Man" for everything. They can tell you are smart because of that. You are ashamed of the slight pride you feel.

You haven't gone unnoticed by the boss either. He thinks your work is great. He offers you a position you know another person of color has been vying for. Your stomach churns when you think of turning down all that money. You could buy a car, get your own place. But you are still ill at ease. After deliberating, you decide that if the other person was more qualified, the boss wouldn't have offered it to you. You accept.

Some of your friends of color understand. Money is tight. Times are hard. Others say you're a backstabber. Others call you an Uncle Tom or a house nigger. You ignore their taunts but it does not stop them from stinging. Your promotion will always be associated with those two phrases and it'll be those two phrases you won't ever

forget each time you are promoted.

You have been at the company for five years now. People have

come and gone. There are not as many people of color as there was

when you started. Of all of the ones present today, you rank the

highest. You are now in a serious relationship and contemplating

buying your first home. You have thought about moving on over the

years. You have even had your resume retyped every six months. Still

you have gone nowhere and you start to think that you might never

leave.

The boss calls you in one day and says he wants to hire some

new blood. He shows you some resumes and asks you to conduct

interviews. He wants you to hire somebody who you could see filling

your shoes one day because soon you would be filling his. You've got a

great future here, he says. You play by the rules, don't cause trouble.

Confidentially, he asks you not to play favorites.

You drill the daylights out of each candidate. You whittled

down the list to two people. One is a person of color and one is not.

You hire the person of color. You tell yourself you did it because the

person was more qualified. In the back of your mind, you know you

hired the person to diversify the executive staff. The boss is surprised

but does not object. Your white friends begin making bets on how long

the person will last. You ask them why. Because, they say, it just
doesn't seem like a good fit.

You decide that maybe it would be best if you separate
yourselves from them. The comments grate on your nerves and make
you edgy. Your significant other points out that you seem tense and
agitated all the time now. When your white friends ask you to hang out
again, you decline. The invitations keep coming and you keep turning
them away. Have we done something to upset you?

Yes, as a matter of fact. You have.

You tell them you don't appreciate the comments they make
about the people of color. You are sick of the questions and the jokes
aren't funny. They have personally offended you several times and
you're tired of it.

Now you have gained a reputation with the white people
around the office for having a bad temper. Things become even more
tense and awkward. You have a confrontation with a coworker who
has accused you of not doing an assignment that this person needed to
complete another assignment. When you delegate, things rarely get
done. The boss is becoming increasingly unhappy with your
department.

You are on edge around your white coworkers. You hear
innuendo and veiled racial comments in everything they say. Your

stomach aches every day. You are chewing antacids like candy. Stress

wears you out. You are caught in the midst of another confrontation

with a coworker who claims he was only joking when he said blacks

needed to go back to Africa if they hated America so much.

You file a complaint with HR but it gets lost. You file another.

You wait for months for some kind of action. None comes. When it is

time for salary increases, yours is rejected. You file another complaint.

After months of filing complaints, you come to work with a box and

without a word you pack your personal belongings and leave.

You don't believe this will be the last time this happens to you.

You don't believe you are the only person this has ever happened to.

You could have stayed there. You could have remained silent and done

nothing for years. Leaving was the right thing to do. Your only regret is

for the person who fills your shoes.

Scream in C Sharp

One morning Jane woke up and screamed. She screamed on the toilet and screamed while she brushed her teeth. She screamed in the shower and she screamed all the way to the bus stop. She climbed aboard the bus and when the driver said, "Good morning" Jane kept screaming and took a seat.

Jane had a dead-end job. At work, Jane screamed and her boss came over to her desk. "What seems to be the trouble?" he asked. But all Jane could do was scream and she kept screaming louder and louder until he walked away.

Jane had a boyfriend that she didn't want anymore. Her boyfriend was frustrated because she wouldn't stop screaming. He said, "If you don't stop this, I'm leaving you." She kept on screaming.

When her throat got dry, she drank water. When it ached, she screamed softly.

She screamed in her sleep.

She screamed every day for a year.

Then one day, she stopped. She woke up and used the toilet and brushed her teeth. She didn't have to work because she lost her

job, so she read books. She became smarter. She didn't have a
boyfriend anymore so she became happier and more confident. She
didn't have much to do in the evenings so she went for walks. Her
weekends were always free so she joined a book club. She got inspired
by books and she wrote stories. She was quite good at it. She sold
stories and eventually wrote a book. The book was a hit.

Jane traveled and lived well. And she grew happier with every
second of every minute of every hour of every day.

Acknowledgements

Thanks to Lulu for offering an awesome service for talented writers to share their passion.

Thanks to my family for helping me stay afloat over the years. My cousins who were more like sisters and my sister who is like a sister, my brothers who make me laugh so hard my stomach hurts, my grandparents who gave me everything I needed and my mother who pushed a miracle into the world and my father who helped out with his chromosomes.

Thanks to my very good friends who were there for me when I couldn't be there for myself, who loved me when I was good and when I was bad.

To my cats, Grace and Oliver, even though you can't read this, your company has been invaluable to me and even though you destroy my place, track litter throughout and lick your genitals when company is over, you're still the coolest cats a girl could have.

To my love, Lamont, you're the best Super Genius a girl could ask for. Thank you for being my friend, being encouraging and supportive and giving me honest to goodness love.